"With this ring, I accept you as my husband."

Gwendolyn had neglected to put the ring on her finger, so she made to rectify that, but Vidar stopped her by covering her hand with his. Gently, he took the ring from her and slid it onto her finger. He didn't say anything, but it felt like he'd claimed her. Just as his ring claimed her finger, he had claimed her as his.

He moved away only to turn back with a sword his Jarl Eirik had given him. It was ornate, with two rubies set into the gilded hilt. He held it out to her lying flat on both of his palms. "I am entrusting this into your care to be given to our firstborn son. May you bear me many."

She nodded and took the sword from him, handing it off to Rodor. "I accept," she said, her voice low enough that only Vidar and Rodor were likely to hear her. "But we never agreed to children."

Now that the ceremony was finished, he relaxed, and even smiled at her when she said that. "I'm looking forward to the challenge, my lady."

They were well and truly wed now.

Author Note

Vidar's story brings to a close the books I've planned in the Viking Warriors series. I've had so much fun exploring the world of Jarl Hegard's sons and their journeys to find love in the unforgiving Viking age. Each book has meant so much to me, but I am especially happy to bring Vidar's story to you.

We first met Vidar in *Enslaved by the Viking* when he was a young teenager working on his older brother's ship. We saw him again when he played reluctant nurse to his ailing and grumpy half brother in *One Night with the Viking*. Now Vidar has shrugged off the weight of his overbearing brothers and has come into his own with his very own love story.

But his journey is anything but what he wants it to be. He's been saddled yet again with another responsibility that he doesn't want: a wife. No longer free to roam the seas, he must take up the responsibility of his wife and her ancestral estate whether he wants it or not. He's in for a surprise, because Gwendolyn isn't in the market for a husband any more than Vidar is for a wife. When these two clash, no one is safe!

I hope you enjoy Gwendolyn and Vidar's story. Please find me on Facebook if you'd like to chat about it at Facebook.com/harperstgeorge. Thank you so much for reading.

HARPER ST. GEORGE

—

THE VIKING WARRIOR'S BRIDE

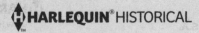

HARLEQUIN® HISTORICAL

Recycling programs
for this product may
not exist in your area.

ISBN-13: 978-0-373-29950-8

The Viking Warrior's Bride

Printed in U.S.A.

Harper St. George was raised in rural Alabama and along the tranquil coast of northwest Florida. It was this setting, filled with stories of the old days, that instilled in her a love of history, romance and adventure. At high school she discovered the romance novel, which combined all those elements into one perfect package. She lives in Atlanta, Georgia, with her husband and two young children. Visit her website, harperstgeorge.com.

Books by Harper St. George

Harlequin Historical

Outlaws of the Wild West

The Innocent and the Outlaw
A Marriage Deal with the Outlaw

Viking Warriors

Enslaved by the Viking
One Night with the Viking
In Bed with the Viking Warrior
The Viking Warrior's Bride

Digital Short Stories

His Abductor's Desire
Her Forbidden Gunslinger

Visit the Author Profile page at Harlequin.com.

For Tara Wyatt,
who was there from the first Viking book.
Thank you!

Chapter One

❧⟨❀⟩❧

The hills had stood like sentinels for the past day
and a half, watching over the boats as they steadily
drew closer. The men's oars cut through the murky
water in a rhythm born from years of practice, a near
silent heave-and-ho that kept the horde advancing
with merciless efficiency. Vidar glared out at those
hills, provoked by their silent taunting. Gwendolyn
of Bernicia lived somewhere in the midst of them.
His enemy. His bride.

He swallowed past the thickening in his throat
that accompanied the thought while his palms itched
to grab his sword, to do *something* to fight the ugly
truth of the wedding that was to come. No matter
how Vidar wished it, he and the men were not here
to do battle. They were here to see him married.

He'd never met Gwendolyn and, if he'd had his
way, he never would. Vidar wasn't supposed to be
the groom in this match arranged by his brother,
Jarl Eirik. Vidar was supposed to be fighting to the

south to expand their territory. The only reason he was here was because the true groom, Magnus, had decided to marry the low-born Saxon woman who'd saved him when he'd been gravely wounded.

Disgust roiled in his stomach and he turned his eyes from the hills. Somewhere in those hills his new home waited. He'd passed the winter trying to reconcile himself with this change of events, but it hadn't worked. He'd fought with Eirik so often that he'd eventually left Eirik's home, spending most of the winter in a camp to the south plotting the spring advancement to take more Saxon territory. It hadn't mattered that Vidar wouldn't be there to take part. It had helped him to feel useful.

Eirik had made this match, aligning his best warrior with the Alveys of Bernicia to help ensure the northern territory was held. There were threats even further north, so the Alvey land would be a barrier to those threats. There had also been some skirmishes with rebellious Danes who lived to the north, but there'd yet to be any evidence of a great band of them. There were the Picts and the Scots further north, but they were small tribes who'd undoubtedly be no match for seasoned Danes. Rather than fighting battles, this move north felt a lot like banishment.

Vidar knew that he would be much more effective leading a group of warriors to battle and adventure in new lands. Protecting this land was the work of old men, not that of a warrior in his prime.

He had years of travel ahead of him yet. He'd die before he lived out his years in these hills tending sheep and crops.

Though the bitter cold of winter had drawn to a close, the days were still short and the sun had long since disappeared behind an endless haze of grey clouds. A slight wind blew in frosty air over those hills along with a feeling he couldn't name. A trepidation he couldn't place. At first he'd thought it had been his own distaste for all that the place represented to him. But Eirik, who led in the first boat, raised his fist high in the air, drawing the line of eight boats to a halt.

A chill crept down Vidar's spine and he leaned forward, his palms on the smooth gunwale of his ship as he scanned the trees on either side of the river. He couldn't find anything amiss. The shores were still, which might have raised alarm except it was still cold enough in the nights that many of the wild animals had already settled down in their dens.

Eirik had hoped they'd make it to their destination by nightfall, but Vidar confessed to a certain relief at not having reached it yet. Another night without a bride was one more night of freedom. Too bad there weren't any women in their group with whom to enjoy it.

'There!' Eirik called back and pointed towards the eastern shore.

Vidar squinted into the gathering dusk and barely made out an opening in the trees. It might be an animal path leading from the river, but it just as well could be a human trail. He sighed and stood up straighter when Eirik's boat made for shore. It looked as if he was to be denied his last night of freedom after all. Very well. He'd meet his bride tonight. It was probably best to sort out the particulars of their arrangement sooner rather than later.

As one the boats glided towards the eastern shore. Eirik's boat reached it first. Two men near the prow jumped over the side, holding the ropes that would guide it to shore. Vidar called out to his own men to get them ready to disembark. Half pulled in their oars and readied themselves to jump overboard, when an arrow whizzed past Vidar's shoulder. There was no warning, simply a hiss of air as it flew past. He would have thought he'd imagined the sensation of the air ruffling his hair if he hadn't caught sight of it from the corner of his eye and watched it disappear into the dark water behind him.

'Halt!' a voice called out from the trees. There was still no sign of people on the shore, but that blasted arrow had come from somewhere. Eirik looked around, startled at the sound of the voice. It appeared no one else had seen the first arrow, but it was followed by another one that landed with a loud *thunk* in the open mouth of the wooden beast adorning Vidar's prow.

'Grab your shields,' Vidar yelled and the men on all the ships hurried to obey the command. The two men on Eirik's ship who had disembarked lunged back on to the boat. Before another arrow came down, the men crouched behind the walls of the ships with their shields above their heads, creating a nearly impenetrable wall of armour.

Vidar stood higher than the others with his own shield before him. He grabbed his sword from the scabbard on his back and held it, ready to jump over the side and fight whoever had dared to attack them. He didn't have to wait long before a row of men stepped out of the trees. They held swords and pikes and wore armour that looked as if it might have been left over from the days of the Romans. Some of the helmets were rusted and tarnished, but many of the breastplates and chainmail looked solid enough. They were not armoured well enough to be the rebel Danes said to inhabit these parts.

Eirik called out to them in the common Saxon tongue and not one of them answered. He tried again in Danish, but there was no response. Vidar hadn't thought they'd travelled far enough north to encounter any Picts or Scots, but he couldn't rule out the possibility that they'd somehow stumbled across a group heading south. Perhaps Vidar's seclusion in the north wouldn't be as dull as he'd originally feared.

Nearly a score of the men had revealed themselves on the shore, but there had to be more if they were bold enough to challenge the group of boats that held over a hundred warriors. A rustling in the trees drew his attention. A high limb on an evergreen shimmied and then the one below it shook and so on as someone appeared to be climbing down. He only caught glimpses of a leather-clad figure until it had moved closer to the ground. The limbs were sparser there and he saw a set of curvy hips drop down from a limb revealing a shapely backside in a pair of leather trousers. The person dropped to the ground and pulled off the crossbow that had been slung across his shoulders. When he walked out of the trees, Vidar noted the length of braided sable hair that fell across a rounded breast that proclaimed the person was not a he at all, but a generously endowed woman. She wore a dark brown tunic that reached mid-thigh, leaving her legs free for doing things such as climbing trees. From what he could see, they were very nice legs. She wore a pair of high boots that laced up to her knees.

Her expression was fierce and unyielding as she walked to stand next to her men—and there was no doubt that the men were hers, rather than her belonging to them. They bristled with respect when she came to a stop beside them and called out, 'I am Gwendolyn of Alvey and you are trespassing on our land. Who are you?' She spoke in the common Saxon tongue though her words held a slight accent he hadn't heard before.

Vidar couldn't help but stare at the woman. His own father had never allowed women to become warriors back home. Though it wasn't an unheard-of custom, Vidar had never fought with one of the shield maidens that other Jarls allowed amongst their warriors. The ones he had seen hadn't been particularly attractive, seeming to take on the sometimes crude and harsh appearance of the men they fought beside. This woman, however, was striking. She was nearly as tall as the men she stood with and, from what he'd seen of her backside when she'd dropped from the tree, had a woman's body. She stood poised beside them, her shoulders back in confidence as she held the crossbow at her side.

And if she spoke true, she was going to be his wife. He stood speechless, unable to form a coherent thought, much less a sentence.

Eirik held up his right hand in greeting, though he kept his sword at the ready in his left hand behind his shield. 'Gwendolyn of Alvey, I am Jarl Eirik of the Danes to the south. Your father and I struck a bargain and we're here to deliver your husband.'

Her posture stiffened. Vidar gathered that the information was displeasing to her and he nearly grinned. At least his nights might be pleasantly occupied if they involved taming the wench.

'I have no need for a husband,' she surprised them all by saying.

Vidar smiled at her impertinence. In all his days of dreading this marriage, he'd never once assumed the woman didn't want to be wed to him. From what he knew of women, they bartered their bodies for position and status all the time. Although he had to admit that this particular woman seemed very different than the ones he generally kept time with. He might have sympathised with her plight had he not been so amused at the turn of events.

For his part, it appeared that Eirik hadn't anticipated this response, because he was a moment in responding. Vidar filled in the silence. 'Perhaps a husband is exactly what you need.'

Her gaze swept over the boats until she found him standing at the prow of his ship. She cast him a scathing glare before turning her attention back to his brother. 'I regret you've come all this way, but my father was mistaken.'

'Where is your father? I'd discuss this with him,' Eirik said.

'My father is dead. He died of natural causes in the autumn.'

Vidar frowned. That only partially explained why she was greeting them herself, but it didn't explain why or how she'd earned the men's respect. They stood as if awaiting her command. A few months wouldn't be enough to solidify her leadership with them.

'I regret to hear of your father's passing. You have our condolences.' Eirik called out. 'The betrothal still stands, however. The agreement was signed by your father and brought back to me by messenger. I'm told by your father's own man that this was as good as a marriage to your people. We must only now go through the formality of a ceremony.'

The woman thought that over for a moment, her

brow furrowing with dismay. She was clearly not any happier with this marriage arrangement than Vidar. 'Where is this man?' She looked over the boats. Some of the shields had lowered so that the men were peeking out with interest at the events unfolding.

'I am here,' Vidar called out with some amusement. He felt the power of her gaze in his gut when it locked on his. The realisation hit him that this woman would be in his life from this day forward. Whether he ultimately decided to go back to fighting rather than stay and manage the manor, she would be there like a shadow in the back of his mind. His responsibility. His burden. *His*.

'You are Magnus.' Her expression was unfathomable. She looked like a queen and he felt the first stirrings of respect well within him.

'I am Vidar. Jarl Eirik's younger brother.'

She didn't waste a moment in arguing the replacement. 'The agreement was for a warrior named Magnus. I won't accept a proxy or a substitution.' She looked at Vidar as if he were a poor substitute at that.

The woman was stunning in her audacity. Vidar couldn't stop the laughter that rolled out of his chest. He nearly doubled over as it tore through him. He'd never seen anyone like her. For all his anger over the winter, the woman didn't want to wed him any more than he'd wanted to wed her. He'd welcome her refusal if he wasn't so certain that Eirik wouldn't stand for it.

'It appears you don't have a choice,' he said when he could finally draw a breath.

Gwendolyn tightened her hands into fists around the wooden frame of the crossbow. Every instinct she possessed urged her to put an arrow through the black heart of the Dane who was laughing at her so hard that he nearly fell out of his ship. Perhaps she should have aimed for him sooner, instead of that grotesque beast of a mast head. If she shot him now, it would no doubt lead to an outright battle. Aside from that, the men would never forgive her taking a life in cold blood, no matter that he was a threat to her in ways she was afraid to face.

She'd been preparing for this day—along with dreading it—ever since her father had confessed on his deathbed to this secret arrangement he'd made with the Danes who controlled the land to the south. Despite her hope that somehow the Danes had forgotten her over the winter, she'd had the men on alert for their arrival since the earth had thawed earlier in the month. When the lookout had come with the news that boats had been spotted that morning, she knew that her time had come and her prayers to be delivered from this unwanted marriage had gone unanswered. She'd actually hoped that these men were not part of Jarl Eirik's fleet and had instead come bent on battle. A fight she could handle. A new husband was a different beast altogether.

Now she had to face the fact that only one of them had come to do battle and it appeared it would be with her. With that in mind she seized on the only piece of information that might save her from the marriage. Turning her gaze back to Jarl Eirik, she said, 'My father told me that Magnus was your second in command and the only man worthy of wedding into our family. If this Magnus has chosen not to honour this agreement, then I am afraid that I will not honour a replacement.'

The Jarl did not answer for a moment. Instead, he gave a long slow look at the men in the seven other boats that had pulled up next to his. There were at least twenty men on each one, while the two in back held a few horses. She allowed herself the tiny sliver of hope that she had saved herself. But then he spoke. 'The agreement called for my most trusted warrior. Magnus was named verbally, but his name was not recorded in the document. Just as your name was not recorded. The text only states that my most trusted warrior is to marry the daughter of Alvey. I have the scroll if you'll allow me to show you.'

She opened her mouth to refuse him, but Rodor stepped forward and placed a hand on her shoulder. She met his shrewd gaze and noted the displeasure there. He'd been her father's man from long before her birth—if anyone knew what her father's wishes had been, it was he. He'd probably even seen the document her father had signed.

'Do not do this thing you're planning, Gwendolyn. If you antagonise your husband now, think of the consequences to yourself later. Think of the consequences to our people. A true leader must put everyone else before himself...or herself.'

Her heart plummeted to land with a thud in her stomach. All this time she had been so certain that something would change, but she realised now that she'd only been fooling herself. It hadn't been certainty at all, but a childish indulgence. Nothing would save her from her fate. Her father had made sure of that before he'd passed by making his wishes known to all the men. They followed her now because she'd earned their respect, but she knew how tenuous that respect was. If she openly thwarted her beloved father's wishes, they'd turn on her. If Jarl Eirik had chosen not to honour the agreement, then that would be one thing; but, if she were the cause of him baulking, that would be another altogether.

The men thought they needed these Danes for protection. Personally, she didn't agree. Aye, the northern tribes were becoming bolder. That was compounded by the rebellious Northmen who'd fled the Danes pushing northward to take Alvey land. They were being squeezed from both sides, yet Gwendolyn was confident that her men could handle things alone. But Jarl Eirik had promised them gold and warriors in exchange for her hand and her father had thought the exchange necessary.

Swallowing her pride, she realised that she'd have to handle this diplomatically, so she nodded to Jarl Eirik. 'You may come on land. Bring your proof and whatever you may need to rest for the evening. We'll see if everything is as you say.'

From the corner of her eye, she saw Rodor nod as he stepped back to his place with the men. The one named Vidar had ceased his laughing, but only to stare at her. She ignored him, training her gaze on Jarl Eirik as he directed his men to disembark. He followed them, his boots splashing in the shallow water at the bank of the river as he jumped out of the boat and walked to shore. He was a tall man, taller than Rodor. His shoulders were broad and his wheat-coloured hair swept down past his shoulders. He was handsome and had a solemn air about him. If he hadn't been her adversary, she saw immediately that she would have liked him.

His younger brother Vidar followed—she wouldn't think of him as her betrothed until it was absolutely unavoidable. When he splashed down from his boat and walked towards shore, she noted that he walked with a swagger that was missing from his older brother's walk. He was of the same height as Jarl Eirik and his hair was a similar shade of blond. It was obvious they were brothers. But the younger one's eyes were insolent and fierce. Gwendolyn very much doubted she would have liked him at all under other circumstances.

'Come,' she said and turned to follow the trail home. She forced down the ache in her throat and blinked back the sting of tears. She had not cried since the day her father had died. She wouldn't allow this Dane to reduce her to shame herself in front of him.

Somehow between now and the night ahead, she'd figure a way out of this marriage. She wouldn't have a man dictate her future to her, especially an enemy stranger.

Chapter Two

The trail was so narrow that they'd been forced to walk in pairs, and Vidar had fallen into step beside his brother. They'd left half of the men behind to guard the boats and the treasure contained within them—the fortune his brother had been forced to part with to secure this marriage. The girl walked before them with a man he'd heard her call by the name Wulf at her side, while the rest of her men followed behind.

'Have you considered that this might be a trap?' Vidar asked, keeping his voice low enough that it wouldn't travel to the others. Not that he believed any of the Saxons knew the Danish tongue, but he'd rather his own men not hear. The evergreen forest towered high above them, nearly blocking what little light there was, leaving it almost too dark to see the trail in front of them. She could be leading them anywhere.

'Aye, but it's not,' Eirik said, his gaze on the trail.

Vidar had to agree that a trap was probably unlikely. As of now, they had the Saxon men outnumbered, but there could be more hiding anywhere along the trail. And their knowledge of the Alveys was nearly non-existent. They could have hundreds of warriors. Yet his brother spoke with such confidence that Vidar was compelled to ask, 'How are you so certain?'

'When I leave, I'm taking nearly half the warriors with me and leaving the gold behind.' Eirik smiled, the white of it breaking through the shadows. 'If she wanted to kill you, she'd do it then when she'd have fewer men to contend with and it would be autumn before I knew about it. Spring before I'd be able to come back to avenge you. It's in her best interest to wait.'

Vidar scoffed and glanced through the tops of the trees, trying to find the sun. 'Many thanks, Brother. I'll look forward to that when you're gone.'

Eirik laughed and clapped him on the shoulder. 'I doubt it'll happen.'

Somehow his brother's 'doubt' wasn't the least bit reassuring. Vidar clenched his jaw and stared at the back of the girl who walked before them. Vidar still had trouble thinking of her as his bride. None of this felt like it was really happening. By tomorrow evening the land they were walking on could very well be his, but he couldn't bring himself to care about it. He wasn't a farmer or a shepherd, or whatever they did up here in this remote place. His destiny was to brave new lands to find new resources and secure his fortune.

No matter what happened on this night or any other, he'd make sure to fulfil that destiny. These people had survived well enough without him. He'd leave as soon as he was able and continue his life as before. Eirik couldn't stop him and, unless he missed his guess, his bride would rather see him go.

Though he'd probably have to get her with child first.

The thought brought his attention back to her. They had been steadily walking up an incline, traversing up the side of the hill, so the girl's backside was at eye level. Her tunic was low enough that it covered the plump flesh, but he could still see it bouncing beneath the fabric, the swells of each cheek working with each step she took. And he remembered vividly how her tunic had been pulled up as she'd come out of the tree, allowing him a view of those rounded curves in her trousers. It could be worse, he reminded himself. Bedding her wouldn't be unpleasant, he decided, and began to anticipate it as the only bright spot in this arrangement. It had been weeks since he'd last lain with a woman.

The flickering of fire up ahead caught his eye and he realised they were coming out of the forest. The trail ended and they walked out into a flat grassland that backed up to a fortress larger than he'd been expecting. The entire settlement was set back into the side of a hill. The river made up the west and north side, blocked off by both a stone wall and sheer drop of several yards. The stone wall continued around the south and east sides of the property, but it was far more vast in both length and height than any of the Saxon walls he'd seen. Inside the wall, set up higher on the hill, were several larger buildings and many smaller ones scattered about them. It was too dark to make out specific details, but he was impressed with what he saw. He'd imagined a few huts around a granary, but this was remarkable. If he wasn't mistaken in the dim light, a few of the buildings looked to be made of the same stone as the wall.

Gwendolyn turned when they reached the wall, her gaze flicking over him before landing on Eirik. 'Welcome to my home, Jarl Eirik.' Vidar noticed that she specifically excluded him from the greeting. Did the girl think goading him was in her best interest? He smiled, already warming to the idea of taming her.

'Many thanks, Lady Gwendolyn. I'm impressed with your fortifications,' Eirik answered. The wall was well over two men high. Torches were set at even intervals along the top of the wall, giving a little bit of light to the early evening.

'Thank you. My grandfather was an intelligent man with the gift of foresight. He had this built back when we'd only heard talk about the invaders.'

She didn't say the word 'invaders' with malice, but her gaze slid over to Vidar just the same. It appeared the lady only considered *him* the invader and not Eirik. Did she not realise that he would not be here if it weren't for Eirik? Vidar very nearly snorted, but managed to hold himself in check. There'd be plenty of time after the wedding to put her in her place.

'A wise man indeed,' Eirik agreed, his gaze traversing the wall. 'Has it held up well to attack?'

'Aye,' the girl said, raising her chin a notch in pride.

'It's never fallen,' said the man at her side. 'It's been tested, but not once has it failed us.' He appeared old enough to be the girl's father. His dark hair was streaked with grey at the temples, while his beard had patches of silver. He carried himself with the same pride of ownership as the girl.

'Jarl Eirik, this is my father's man, Rodor. He knows everything there is to know about Alvey. He was born here and has the charge of our warriors just as his father before him.'

Vidar watched them exchange greetings and offered his own arm for Rodor. The man hesitated, his gaze faltering for a moment as he glanced at Gwendolyn. It was true that the girl had led the men below, but Vidar hadn't been sure if it had been a scheme. Part of something she'd concocted to make a show of her power in their first meeting. But that look spoke volumes. This older man, who'd clearly had the trust and respect of her father, trusted her. Not only that, but he gave deference to her wishes. Interesting.

She gave an almost imperceptible tilt of her head that Rodor took for consent. Only then did the man clasp Vidar's arm in the same grip he'd shared with the Jarl and exchange a greeting. Gwendolyn turned her head away as if she couldn't bear to see Vidar acknowledged in any way other than that of an enemy or threat. When he let go of the man's arm, she turned and led them all to the main gate, which had been thrown open in welcome. Although it didn't feel like much of a welcome when they walked inside.

Vidar had to suppress a shiver of trepidation as he passed through the gates. The men inside had been alerted to their arrival and stood on either side of the entrance. Though they were not holding their weapons, swords, axes, and knives were stowed at the waistbands and across their backs. He had to wonder if the girl commanded them as easily as she did Rodor.

She walked through the warriors and they parted for her as if she were their queen. Vidar realised that his original assessment of her had been hasty. This was no token respect she was given. These men respected her because somehow she had earned it.

Vidar ground his molars together, already anticipating the battle of wills ahead. It wouldn't be fought with weapons. It would be more subtle, and fought with words and deeds. He'd have to wrest their respect away from her and earn it for himself.

* * *

'The Danes have come.' Gwendolyn could barely say the words before she pressed a hand to her mouth, as if they'd cut her lips on their way out.

'Aye. I've heard. The news spread fast once their ships were spotted.' Her older sister, Annis, closed the door to Gwendolyn's bedchamber and swept her into her arms.

Gwendolyn allowed herself a moment of weakness and took comfort in the embrace. Her knees had been weak since the moment she'd climbed out of that tree and met the Northmen face to face. Her fear had only got worse as she'd led the men to her home. Now that they were inside, drinking her ale and helping themselves to her meat, she'd barely made it to her chamber before the fear overtook her.

She'd heard talk about the Danes ever since she could remember. They were large and unkempt with the slovenly mannerisms of barbarians. Her only real dealings with them before now were that band of misfit Danes who terrorised the countryside. They didn't belong to this group of men, though. They were rebels. Rumours were that only a portion of them were Danes with the rest of the group being made up of outcasts from the Picts, Scots, and God knew who else. During that battle, she'd been too grief stricken and intent on avenging her brother's death to notice much about them.

What frightened her so much about these Danes who'd all but taken over Northumbria was that they weren't unkempt and slovenly at all. They were dignified and ordered. Jarl Eirik appeared just as aristocratic as her own father had. The men as a group carried themselves with pride and poise. When she looked into Vidar's eyes, she saw intelligence and cunning, not the look of a barbarian she'd been expecting. She could handle a bloodthirsty animal much easier than a calculating nobleman, particularly one bent on claiming her for marriage and taking her property.

Her bedchamber was the only place she could indulge her emotions, even if only for a moment. And Annis was the only person she trusted enough to allow her to see her as she really was. With Annis she didn't have to appear strong or brave. She buried her face in the crook of Annis' shoulder and took a deep breath to calm her racing heart. However, nothing could stop her hands from shaking as she put them around her sister's shoulders.

'Are they so awful?' Annis asked, her voice low as if the Danes already had ownership of everything and any words spoken against them were blasphemy.

Gwendolyn nodded. 'More awful than I had imagined.'

'What of your...husband?' She hesitated on the last word as if trying to find another way to say it. But there was no other way. Gwendolyn feared that she was as good as wed to him.

'Any man who is not Cam is horrible. But that man is worse than horrible.' Gwendolyn took another deep breath and pulled herself up to her full height, which was a few inches taller than her tiny sister. Though Gwendolyn had two older sisters, she'd always been the tallest and the most active of the three. When her sisters were content to allow their mother to lead them in lessons in embroidery and the proper running of a household, Gwendolyn had followed their older brother Cedric everywhere. Eventually her parents had consented and he'd allowed her to join in with the weaponry and fight training given to the boys her age. It was because of him that she was more accurate with the crossbow than any of the men and could hold her own with the longbow.

In a way, it was because of Cedric that she was in this awful predicament. If he'd not been killed in battle, along with Cam—her betrothed—then she'd not be faced with marriage to a Dane.

'I understand that you still mourn Cam. We all do.' Annis tucked a strand of hair behind Gwendolyn's ear. 'But the Danes are only men. They can't possibly be that awful.'

Gwendolyn turned from her sister and hurried across the room to the shelves where she kept the important documents that had belonged to her father. In preparation for the marriage, Gwendolyn had moved into the master's chamber. With her brother dead, Annis married to a lowly farmer with no lofty aspirations and her other sister comfortably ensconced in the abbey and devoted to a life of prayer, there

was no one left to be master except for the man
Gwendolyn eventually married. She only hoped it
wouldn't be this Dane.

Grabbing the small chest from the shelf, she sat it
on the table and opened the lid to pull out the scroll
her father had hidden away. It was the one that had
given her to that heathen. 'They are that terrible,
Annis,' she said. 'His name is Vidar and you can't
even imagine how he looks at me. It's not the same
way Eadward looks at you.' Eadward fairly wor-
shipped her sister. He'd looked at her as if he could
see no one else since they were children. 'It's as if
he already owns me and is taking measure of my
worth.'

She shook her head as she unrolled the scroll,
nearly ripping it in her haste to find the name Magnus. If Magnus was the one named in the document,
and not Vidar, then she wouldn't have to honour this
ridiculous agreement that her father had made in
haste and desperation. This was nothing more than
her father's misplaced fear. He'd been afraid to die
without seeing her cared for, not realising that she
didn't need to be cared for. She could care for herself, the estate and all the land between the north
and Northumbria without a man at her side.

'Damn and blast,' she murmured as her gaze ate
up the words on the page.

'Gwendolyn! We can get through this without
blasphemy,' Annis admonished her before turning her attention back to the scroll, squinting at the

words. She'd never taken to learning the written word as her other siblings had. Her lips moved silently as she struggled to make sense of the markings. Finally, she gave up. 'Oh, just tell me what it says.'

'They've brought a man named Vidar to marry me, but Father explicitly said that the man's name was Magnus. The Jarl Dane says that the agreement only called for his best man and a specific man had not been named. Therefore, he could substitute whomever he wanted.' Gwendolyn dropped into the chair behind her as nausea rolled in her stomach, the scroll forgotten on the table. 'It appears he's correct. There is no Magnus named in the agreement.'

Annis grabbed her hand in silent support. Gwendolyn squeezed her fingers, but the gesture that was so familiar did nothing to bring her peace this time. She was well and truly bound to that barbarian. An image of his smirking face rose up in her mind and she shook her head to clear it. This was not the future she had planned for herself.

She felt like throwing a tantrum that would have left her five-year-old self in complete and utter awe. However, she realised that would get her absolutely nowhere.

Instead of giving in to the impulse, she rolled up the scroll again and put her arm around Annis. Vidar—even thinking his name was distasteful. She shook her head and said, 'If legalities won't save me, then I'll have to make him cry off.'

'How on earth will you do that, Gwendolyn? What man would say no to Alvey?'

Gwendolyn closed her eyes as dread settled like a lump in her belly. She knew she was getting desperate if she thought she could make him turn around and leave. 'I don't know. Your Eadward said no. Father would've given it to him after Cedric's death.'

Annis laughed. 'You know as well as I that Eadward is happiest on his farm. He goes whole days without so much as a word to anyone. He would not be happy as a ruler.' Then she sobered and took Gwendolyn's hand. 'Perhaps I should've said what man who's travelled weeks and weeks to find you and claim Alvey as his own would turn away now?'

And that was the crux of it. He wouldn't. He wouldn't have come all this way to simply turn around now. Even worse was her strong suspicion that even if he did, Jarl Eirik would only find someone to replace him. Despite what Vidar might want for himself, she knew that Jarl Eirik wanted this land as a barrier between himself and the tribes to the north. And he needed that to happen before the Saxons to the south claimed it for their own. Or that's how her father had explained it to her from his deathbed.

Gwendolyn just wanted to be left alone and for Alvey to be secluded from the kings to the south and the tribes to the north.

'You could very well be right, Annis, but I have to try something. How would you feel if Eadward had been taken from you and a strange barbarian forced upon you?'

Annis nodded and her eyes filled with so much sadness and pity that it hurt Gwendolyn to look at them. 'I'm so sorry,' she said, her eyes filling up with tears. 'It should be me, not you. I'm the oldest and this should be my burden.'

'Oh, Annis.' Gwendolyn pulled her into a hug, suddenly ashamed that she'd allowed her own fears to make her sister feel guilty. 'It's not your fault. I suppose it's not anyone's fault.' As much as she wanted to find someone to blame, it was simply the way things were. 'I'll have to figure things out.'

Annis nodded and drew back, wiping at her nose with a kerchief she'd drawn from her sleeve. 'You will, Gwendolyn. I have great faith in you. You always figure out a way.'

Chapter Three

Gwendolyn had not figured out a way. Despite her best efforts, she was stuck in this marriage arrangement. Rodor and Jarl Eirik stood at the table where their tankards of ale had been pushed to the side and the two scrolls stretched out before them. One of them was from the chest in her chamber, and the other had been produced by Jarl Eirik. She could tell from her seat at the head of the table that they were identical even before Rodor stood back and gave her a solemn nod.

Tightening her grip on her tankard, she tossed back the rest of the ale and contemplated how many cups she could drink that night. If she finished off an entire pitcher, would it be enough to make her forget that this was her life now? That these men who sat at her table would be here to stay? That that man…Vidar…would be her husband? Nay, she sincerely doubted there was enough ale in Alvey to make her forget.

'Well, Lady Gwendolyn, as you can see the documents support my earlier statement. I'm within my rights to replace Magnus with Vidar.' Jarl Eirik pushed back from where he'd been leaning over the documents to stand beside Rodor.

For all his bluster earlier, Rodor kept his hand resting lightly on the sword at his hip. It was a casual pose, but she realised it for the support it was. If she commanded it, he'd turn on the Danes. He'd hate every moment of it, but he'd do it.

Her gaze went down the length of the table and then further around the large chamber. The candles flickered overhead and a large fire burned in the hearth, illuminating the room while keeping the corners in shadow. All eyes had turned to her and there was a tension in the room that had rarely been present in a home that was so well cared for. She counted roughly three score of the Danes. Her own men numbered nearly that many, but there were more lingering outside. Their women were suspiciously absent from the great chamber on this night, leaving only herself and Annis.

If Gwendolyn called for a fight, then her men would eventually overpower the Danes, though not without some loss of life. If they moved fast enough, they'd even be able to attack the Danes still left in their ships. Though it was anyone's guess if the Danes would move fast enough to escape on their ships. If they did escape, then they'd return to avenge their Jarl. It might be weeks or months, but they'd come back with hellfire. She was confident in Alvey's ability to withstand a siege, but she had no real idea of how many Danes they'd come back with. It would be a risk.

If she went through with the marriage and allowed Jarl Eirik to leave in peace, she'd still be able to attack the men he left behind. A year…maybe more would pass before he realised something was amiss, but eventually he'd send a contingent of men and he'd see what she had done. Then Alvey would still need to contend with the hellfire he'd rain down upon them. And she'd have to face the fact that she'd killed her own husband in cold blood.

Neither option was very appealing. Both of them would lead to the deaths of at least a few of her men. What Rodor had said earlier rang true. A true leader must put everyone else first.

Swallowing against the lump in her throat, she said, 'Aye, Jarl Eirik, I can see that you are within your rights.' She studiously avoided looking at Vidar, who was still seated near his brother's side. He'd yet to weigh in with his opinion and she couldn't take the smirk she was sure to find on his face. 'I'd like to know why the substitution was necessary.' Would Magnus have been any better than Vidar?

The Jarl inclined his head as if he'd expected the enquiry, but his grimace made her think he wasn't completely pleased with having to relay the information. 'Magnus is the leader of Thornby, our most powerful settlement. He was injured in battle and a

Saxon woman took him in and healed him. After his stay in her village, he was able to quell a rebellion by the Saxons and decided to marry the woman. I felt his influence there was necessary for peace in the area.'

Gwendolyn wondered if the woman had agreed to the marriage, or if she'd had it thrust upon her, but she kept silent.

Jarl Eirik continued, 'I chose Vidar to replace him because I trust him to see to Alvey's protection. He's learned everything he knows at my side.'

Finally, Gwendolyn allowed her gaze to move to Vidar, who was sitting at the table. He leaned back in his chair with an ankle propped on one knee, almost indolent in his regard of the situation. There was nothing for Gwendolyn to do but nod her acceptance of the Jarl's explanation.

Jarl Eirik smiled. It crinkled the sun-bronzed skin around his eyes and made him seem genuinely good natured rather than smug. 'Good, then let's move ahead to talk about the ceremony.' He took his seat and reached for the ale he'd pushed to the side. Rodor walked around the table and sat down across from him, taking the vacant seat next to Annis. 'Unless you'd prefer a substitution of your own?' he asked after Rodor had seated himself.

'What do you mean?' Gwendolyn asked.

'Your father calls for his daughter to wed my best man. He doesn't specify which one.' Jarl Eirik's gaze wandered across the table to where Annis sat with her back ramrod straight. Her fingers were laced together in front of her, but her knuckles had turned white because she'd clasped them together so hard. The colour had drained from her face as soon as she'd sat down at the table with the men. She was obviously afraid. Gwendolyn was suddenly very glad that she was the one who had to deal with this. If it were Annis, she feared her sister wouldn't survive it.

Forcing a smile, Gwendolyn said, 'I'm afraid that I'm the only daughter available for the task.'

'Then I'm a lucky man.' Vidar spoke for the first time since they'd started this meeting. His voice was deep but smooth and pleasing to the ear. It matched his appearance. He was well groomed with fine features and she suspected that he left a trail of admirers wherever he went. But it would take more than surface charm to win him any favours here.

Gwendolyn met his gaze and found that he was indeed as amused as she'd thought he might be. Though he wasn't smirking, his eyes were lit with some inner light that told her he found the situation amusing. Of course he found her discomfort amusing. He was clearly a barbarian.

'You're more beautiful than I expected,' Vidar explained, raising a brow. She recognised it for the challenge that it was rather than a compliment to her appearance.

'You're younger than I expected,' she countered. He *was* younger than she'd thought he would be, she realised as she saw him clearly for the first time.

She'd prepared herself for an older man, someone like Rodor. Jarls were supposed to be older men. But Jarl Eirik didn't appear to be that old and his brother was obviously quite a few years younger. He was probably only scarcely older than her own twenty winters. Although there was nothing about him that said anything other than full-grown man. His chest was broad and she could tell from the way the fabric of his tunic hugged his shoulders that his muscles were well developed.

'Young and virile,' he quipped, somehow putting extra emphasis on the word *virile*. 'Isn't that what was called for in the agreement?'

She felt heat rise on her cheeks. An image of his nude body flashed through her mind and there was no place in this discussion for that.

Jarl Eirik cleared his throat, clearly uneasy with the direction the conversation had taken. 'I can have Rodor, or someone else of your choosing, taken down to the ships and shown the bride price to reassure you.'

Gwendolyn nodded, having trouble getting that virile thought to stay out of her head. 'In the morning will be soon enough.'

Jarl Eirik inclined his head. 'Then we should speak of the actual ceremony. I must apologise, but I'd have it take place sooner rather than later. I'm needed at home.'

Her mind raced with a hundred excuses. If she could put it off for years, then she would. But much to her surprise, Annis spoke first. 'The ceremony should take place with the new moon.'

Gwendolyn stared at her sister, certain that she had imagined the interruption from the meek woman. But then her sister spoke again, her gaze on the Jarl. 'I know my sister doesn't put much faith in the stars, but I believe they tell us more than most of us ever realise. Our parents' marriage and even my own marriage began with a new moon, and I believe hers will be most fortuitous if allowed to follow the tradition.'

Gwendolyn looked at her sister, confused by what amounted to a betrayal. Annis knew how she felt about this marriage. The new moon was in three days. Three days to prepare to become that Dane's wife. Three years wouldn't be long enough to prepare for that. Before she could utter an objection, Jarl Eirik's smile broadened. 'Perfect. If your family has a tradition, then I most certainly do not want to be the one to break it.'

Annis smiled and blinked as if she was a little stunned that her suggestion had been accepted. 'Wonderful. That gives us three days to plan and prepare a feast.'

Gwendolyn opened her mouth to protest, but Rodor kicked her leg underneath the table and she ended up swallowing a yelp of pain. Her gaze again found Vidar's across the table and she was surprised to find that he frowned, his brows pulled together as his gaze narrowed on hers. In the light of the candles flickering overhead, she realised that his eyes were the clearest shade of blue she'd ever seen. Not grey, or flecked with green, but clear like the bluest sky. And at that moment there wasn't a speck of kindness in them. She didn't understand what a life with him would mean for her and that sent a wave of anxiety tumbling through her. Would he be cruel? Would he expect her to be a wife like Annis? Someone sweet and biddable and unconcerned with things outside her own home? Would he try to take away the only life she'd ever known?

'In three days, then,' he agreed, sending her heart plummeting to her stomach.

Perhaps it was possible that he didn't want this marriage either. His attitude made her think he wasn't thrilled with the arrangement. If she talked to him, perhaps he'd agree that the marriage should be in name only.

It was her last hope, but something about him... something about the way he looked at her made her think she wouldn't be successful.

The preparations for the wedding feast began the next morning. Annis had sent a messenger off to her farm to fetch Eadward who would bring goats for the celebration. The hunters had been sent to bring venison and the fishermen were at the river to bring fish to the table. The servants began preparing the pork over the roasting fires.

Gwendolyn had barely slept the night before.

She'd spent part of the night tossing and turning in her bed and the rest of the night pacing around her chamber. There was nothing for it. She was well and truly obliged to marry this Dane. Vidar and Jarl Eirik had already been at her table when she'd emerged from her chamber the next morning. She'd barely been able to bring herself to look at either one of them. After a quick breakfast, Jarl Eirik took her to the ships so that she could verify that the payment he'd brought was sufficient.

He didn't call it payment. He called it *mundr*. It was the bride price her father had demanded from him. Whatever its proper name, it was the gold, jewels and horses that Jarl Eirik had paid for the privilege of having his man marry her. Apparently the barrels and chests were her worth. She wasn't worth a coin more or a jewel less. Her stomach churned as she looked it over.

Seeing it made the betrothal suddenly seem real and it made her think of her first betrothal. Cam had asked her father for her hand on the eve of her seventeenth year. As Rodor's son, he had nothing but the wealth his family had earned working for her family. He had his sword arm, his strong mind and his friendship with her brother that he'd use to support them and their eventual children. There'd been no talk of gold exchanging hands. She'd always known Cam and her father had approved of him. That was the way it was meant to be. These strangers were not supposed to be here.

Closing her eyes, she turned away from the treasure. It would do no good to think of the past. A quick glance at Rodor found him looking at her, the sober expression on his face seeming to repeat his warning of the previous day.

'Think of the consequences to our people. A true leader must put everyone else before himself...or herself.'

'Everything appears to be in order,' she said.

Rodor nodded. 'It does. You honour us with your *mundr*. I accept in place of her father.'

Gwendolyn bit her tongue lest she dispute him. As if they had any choice in accepting the payment. As if the Jarl had any intention of 'honouring' her with the payment. He wanted to expand his holdings and this marriage was the only way to do that. For generations the Alveys had existed comfortably in the north with no need for such arrangements.

But that era had come to an end and it was time to accept that.

Drawing herself up to her full height, she forced herself to nod in acknowledgement of the gift and Rodor's acceptance. 'Thank you, Jarl Eirik.' The words tasted bitter on her tongue and nearly choked her on their way out, but she said them because that was her role here as Lady of Alvey. She would not allow these Danes to take that away from her.

Rodor continued speaking with the Jarl to make arrangements for unloading it as well as where the rest of the Danes could make camp. She waited as long as she could before making her excuses about needing to see to feast preparations and leaving. She stalked up the hill, her breath coming in short huffs as she made it to the front gate of her home.

Annis had the preparations well underway so there was no need for Gwendolyn's help. Instead, she stormed directly to the practice yard. The warriors spent every morning sparring and she was in need of her sword to work off her anger and frustration. She practically ran to the yard, which was on the back side of the granary. Yet when she turned the corner, she skidded to a halt because Vidar was standing there with his sword strapped to his back, calling out orders to the men. *Her* men.

He had two score of them lined up in rows of two facing each other. Each of them stood in squares drawn off on the ground with sticks or lines of small stones. At his command, they began sparring with their swords and struggling not to step out of the box. His own men, the Danes, lazed around the edges of the sparring field, watching with amusement.

'What are you doing?' she asked before she could think to stop herself, rushing towards them. As she ran, some of the men had already started tripping over the walls of their boxes, hitting the ground with groans as they fell outside their designated spaces.

Vidar spared her a glance over his shoulder before he went back to instructing the men. 'Good warriors never lose ground. You must learn to fight without backing away from your enemy. Get up and try again.'

'What are you doing to them?' she asked. 'You'll have them injuring themselves.'

The corner of his mouth tipped up in that smirk that was becoming all too familiar, but he didn't look at her as he watched the two warriors nearest him battling each other. 'Then it will help them to learn.' When the smaller of the two engaged in the sparring contest stepped backwards, Vidar sharply rebuked him. 'Never step backwards from an armed opponent.' The man responded by holding his ground with his feet, but he bent backwards as he locked swords with his opponent who was clearly stronger. The smaller man wasn't able to push the stronger man back.

'What good is a warrior who is injured?'

'He'll be smarter for it,' Vidar answered. Without looking at her again, he walked away from her and between the groups of men, offering critique where he thought it necessary.

Despite the obvious fact that Vidar was younger than half of them, he commanded them with the authority of a seasoned leader. He wore a leather tunic that left his arms bare so that his shoulder and arm muscles bulged as he gestured. He was definitely stronger than most of them, despite his youth.

Rage prickled her skin, washing over her in a sweep that left her skin hot and tight. It wasn't only because he'd taken over their training without consulting with her or Rodor. It was that he did it so effortlessly, as if he was accustomed to giving orders and having them obeyed. As if it was already his right to have command of the warriors when they weren't even married yet. What made it even worse was that her warriors were listening to him as if he *was* right in all of those assumptions.

'Halt!' Her voice rang out over the sparring field with authority.

Vidar whipped his head around to look at her, the smirk and swagger he wore so easily wiped from his face. She had to fight to keep herself from smiling, but she wouldn't stoop to his level. The men closest to her stopped their sparring, but the pairs further away continued. She called out halt again just as one of the men fell over his barrier and stumbled to the ground. The others who hadn't heard her clearly before heard her this time and stood down with their weapons.

'This is not how we train.' She spoke to all of them, but her gaze settled on Vidar.

'Perhaps it's not how they were trained before, but it's how they'll train going forward,' Vidar said, crossing his arms over his chest. He levelled her with a glare that was as cold as it was hot with anger. She had no idea how the two ideas could exist in the same gaze, but he managed to pull it off.

'That's not for you to decide.'

That was met with a murmur of voices that made her realise the Danes were watching the display from the side of the field. Behind him, the men who'd been lounging in the grass rose to their feet to watch. Realising that she was quickly making their spat a spectacle for all to see, she inclined her head in the only conciliatory gesture she could muster. 'Let us talk privately.'

Vidar glared at her. His blue eyes were fierce as he stared her down as if he'd not be sorry to see her engulfed in flames where she stood. 'After the sparring session is over.'

She clenched her teeth against the harsh words that threatened to spew out whether she wanted them to or not. Despite that he was in the wrong, she was ever vigilant of her role as peacekeeper amongst her men. It wouldn't do to antagonise Vidar more than she already had, but neither would it be wise to allow him to disrespect her in front of her men. She'd worked too hard to earn their respect—particularly after Cedric's death—to risk losing it now.

'The sparring session is over now.' She made certain that her voice was loud and clear so that it would carry to the Danes at the edges of the field.

Vidar dropped his arms to his sides, his hands clasped into fists. If it was possible, a near tangible wave of apprehension moved through her warriors as silence descended.

Her heart pounded wildly in her chest, but it wasn't from fear. For the first time since these Danes had arrived on her land, she saw an end, a release, to the impotent rage that had been building inside her. Her heart beat with anticipation of meeting him head on.

The sound of a bell ringing shattered the silence. Gwendolyn blinked to break the spell of the tension and looked away from Vidar to the source of the sound. The bell was hung from a wooden brace near the hall's entrance. It rang three times during the day. To signal the beginning of morning chores for the warriors, to signal the start of afternoon chores and to call the men to the evening meal. Morning chores for the warriors began after their training. Gwendolyn had been so lost in the battle of wills with Vidar that she'd lost all track of the time.

But as she looked towards the bell, she saw Rodor standing beside it, leaving her to wonder if he'd rang it to end the confrontation. If the disapproval etched deeply into his features was an indication, that's exactly what had happened.

Her warriors didn't move a muscle. They stood in their places, watching her and Vidar until the last strains of the ringing had died out. 'Go about your work,' she said in a quiet voice.

For a moment no one moved and then eventually, one by one, they slowly filed away, leaving the sparring field. The last to leave was Wulf. The Danes at the edges of the field hadn't left, but their postures relaxed and a few even sat on their haunches, though they hadn't looked away. Vidar hadn't looked away, either. He stared her down with that cold savagery that only he could manage to pull off.

When all of her men had gone away, he took the few steps that would put him in front of her. In a low voice laced with steel, he said, 'You will not defy me.'

'I have not defied you…yet.'

Chapter Four

The woman hadn't so much as blinked at a tone that made most men tremble. With her shoulders squared and her chin raised, Gwendolyn of Alvey stared him down. Her eyes shimmered like deep blue pools beneath the long fringe of her lashes.

The woman was mad. Everyone had seen how she'd stormed out on to the sparring field and tried to usurp his authority. There was no denying it and the fact that she tried to deny it only made him angrier. 'You came out here with the implicit goal of interfering in my work.'

She gave a quick nod of her head. 'Aye, because your *work* was interfering with the training of my warriors.'

'Ah, I see your confusion.' He smiled as it became clear to him where the misunderstanding lay. 'They are my warriors now. I was training *my* warriors and *you* interfered.'

If he'd have struck her across the face, he couldn't

imagine her becoming any angrier. Her cheeks flushed red and he had to admit that it made her even more attractive. Her eyes flashed with heat and she drew herself up to stand even straighter. It was only then that he realised how tall she was for a woman. The top of her head reached his chin. 'These men are not *your* warriors.' She was so angry that her voice shook.

'The agreement your father signed makes you mine along with all that comes with you.'

She swallowed, as if only remembering that pesky document. 'Not yet. There has been no wedding. We haven't spoken the words.'

'Recall the words of the Jarl—your Jarl now— from last night. You became mine with the signing. It is binding and legal and the words left to be spoken are only ceremony. I could bed you now and no man would stand in my way.'

'If you try to bed me now there would be no need for a man to stand in your way, because I would fight you myself.'

She really was unlike any woman he'd ever met. She was full of fire and a wildness that drew him in. He had no doubt that she would fight him at every turn and for some reason he was starting to enjoy it. Some long-hidden part of him admired her strength and a tiny thread of respect wound its way through him. He grinned and felt the tension leave his shoulders as he settled into verbally sparring with her. 'There's no need to fight me. I'm content to wait. It's only three nights.'

Her jaw tightened as she clenched her teeth. 'I will never submit to you.'

He had no doubt that she meant the words now, but he had every confidence in being able to overcome her resistance. She'd come to see that he was in command now. Not her. And she'd realise her new place in this world. He'd met warriors like her before. They came under his command and saw his youth as something to be challenged, but they didn't realise he'd been on a ship with one brother or another from the time of his tenth winter. He had more experience than most of them.

He'd overcome them and he had confidence that he'd change her mind as well. 'Then I look forward to taming you.'

She wanted to strike him, he could see it in her eyes, but much to her credit she didn't. Instead, she took a step back and took in a deep breath, running her palms down her tunic to smooth out imaginary wrinkles in a visible attempt to calm herself. Finally, she said, 'Then you'll be disappointed. I look forward to fighting you at every attempt.' Then she walked off across the sparring field from the direction she'd come, her back as straight as the blade of his sword.

Her legs were long and lean, eating up the distance with ease. He'd bet they were just as shapely as the lightly muscled curve of her shoulder that he could make out beneath the lightweight wool covering it. Her entire body seemed firm and strong. Yet, it was the sway of her hips that called his gaze as he watched her go. They were pleasantly rounded, as were her buttocks from what he could tell. He found her body appealing. Firm and soft all at the same time. The wedding night would be interesting.

With a smile on his lips, he walked to the edge of the sparring field to gather his men for their training. Since they'd been travelling the past few weeks, they'd been unable to train. It would be a nice change and work off some frustrations for him. He hadn't actually meant to take over the training of her warriors. The Saxons had already been on the field when he'd arrived with his own men and they'd been doing it wrong. Was he supposed to simply stand there and watch them train inefficiently?

'Enough lying around. Get to work,' he called to his men, sending them grumbling on to the field.

'Looks like you've got your work cut out for you with that one,' said Rolfe as he slowly got to his feet, his gaze on Gwendolyn's retreating figure.

Vidar had known Rolfe since they both were boys. They'd been on nearly every adventure together and Vidar counted himself lucky that his friend had agreed to come with him to this remote corner of the world. Vidar had given his men the choice of coming north or staying to the south to battle, and he'd been pleased when all of them had chosen to follow him. Following his friend's gaze to the woman's back, Vidar nodded. 'I think you're right. I have to admit I'm looking forward to the challenge. I'd assumed she'd be a biddable wife.'

Rolfe threw his head back and laughed. 'By the gods, man, why would you assume that? Have you ever met a biddable wife?'

Vidar frowned. He wanted to say that of course he had, but the truth was that he wasn't certain. He'd never had any women in his life to speak of. His mother had died and he couldn't remember her. His older sisters had all moved away once they'd become wives. Growing up, some of the slaves in his father's home had been women, but they'd been shadows in the background who worked to make the household run efficiently. He'd met many women in his travels, but they'd all been passing amusements easily left behind with a trinket for their trouble.

Now that he thought of it, Eirik's wife Merewyn was the only wife he knew. Vidar had seen them argue before, but never for long before either Eirik would sweep her up into his arms and take her to their chamber, or their voices would lower at the table and he couldn't hear them anymore. Either way, they worked out their differences and Vidar had assumed it was because Eirik had reminded her of her place.

He shrugged off his thoughts. It didn't matter that he hadn't met a biddable wife. It only mattered that his wife would be biddable, because he had no intention of indulging her in anything else. 'She'll be obedient soon enough,' Vidar said to his friend, shrugging out of his harness and unsheathing his sword.

'You honestly believe that, don't you?' Rolfe eyed him as if he were daft.

Vidar held his sword up to the meagre light, silently cursing the absence of sunlight in this dark land. If the grey light could be believed, the blade was due for a polishing. 'Of course. Why wouldn't I?'

Rolfe only shook his head. 'I blame this on the fact that you've never kept a woman in your bed for more than a few nights at a time. If you keep them around a little longer, you start to learn little things about how to keep them happy.'

Vidar laughed. 'That's the difference between you and me, my friend. I don't have to work so hard to keep them happy.'

Rolfe swung at him, but Vidar was ready for him and ducked out of the way, turning in a full circle to bring his sword around. Rolfe had already jumped back out of the way, as Vidar had expected he would. This wasn't the first time they'd come to friendly blows.

'Vidar.' Eirik called his name, drawing their mock battle to a stop.

When Vidar looked over to see his brother striding across the field, Rolfe laughed again and slapped him on the back. 'May the gods be with you, Brother.' Then he trotted out on to the sparring field, leaving Vidar alone to face what appeared to be the wrath of his brother. Eirik's brows were drawn together in a deep frown.

'Vidar, what have you done?'

Vidar made a show of looking around the sparring field. His men had already cleared the field of debris and had paired off, sparring with their swords and knives. They had no need of barricades to keep them in tiny boxes, because they'd come of age training to never retreat in a single-opponent battle. It was a feat that required superior upper body strength, which helped them be successful.

'The men are sparring,' he answered and sheathed his sword, as it appeared this conversation might take up more of his time.

Eirik grumbled and raked a hand over the back of his neck. 'What happened with the girl?'

'The girl? You mean the woman who wanted to rip my head off? She had an issue with the way I was training the men.'

'The Saxon men?'

'Aye.' Vidar inclined his head, irritated that he was being subjected to this questioning. After his talk with his lovely betrothed, he had a lot of aggression that he wanted to work off on the field. 'What of it?'

'You cannot come here and simply take over. From what I can gather, their warriors are the girl's responsibility along with Rodor,' Eirik explained.

'Perhaps they were, but they won't be any longer. I'll challenge Rodor to see if he's worthy of the post, but no wife of mine will lead warriors. She'll be Lady of this land. She'll do things that a Lady should do.'

Much to Vidar's surprise, Eirik let out a laugh that rumbled up from deep in his chest. 'And tell me, Brother, what are the things a Lady should do?'

Again, Vidar was at a loss. What did Merewyn do with herself all day? For the life of him, he didn't have an answer. She saw to the needs of the children she'd borne his brother and she generally called out orders for meal preparation; but if she did anything else, he hadn't the slightest notion what it was. He shrugged. 'Anything she wants as long as she leaves the warriors and the battles to me. I'll gladly stay out of her way, as long as she stays out of mine.'

Eirik looked at him for a long moment before his lips ticked up in a grin and he shook his head. 'It strikes me that you are profoundly unsuited to marriage.'

Vidar grinned. 'It only strikes you now? I've been telling you that all winter. I never wanted marriage.'

'And yet you will do your duty.' Eirik sobered and fitted him with a level gaze.

'Aye. I always do my duty to you, Brother. You don't have to question where my allegiance lies.'

'I know.' Eirik nodded. 'It's why you would've been my first choice for this marriage. I only chose Magnus because I know you're not ready, but due to the circumstances…here we are. Ready or not.'

Vidar nodded. He'd spent the past few months

coming to terms with that. While he was still bitter, he had come to accept his duty. 'I still feel that Magnus made a mistake. This place was meant for him.' He spread his arms out wide to encompass the entirety of the manor and the village beyond. Magnus was a leader who had flourished building the settlement. He was meant to lead a colony. To defend rather than attack. 'Magnus could've been a king here. And yet he chose a mere settlement and a lowborn Saxon.' Vidar had struggled not to resent his friend for his choice.

'He chose the woman who held his heart,' Eirik said. 'Much as I did.'

'It's not the same. You left our home to come to the Saxon lands and now you live as a king. You bettered your fortune. You still had adventure. You didn't give it all away.'

'Is that all that matters to you?' Eirik narrowed his eyes at him. 'Adventure? Treasure? Battle? What's left after all of that? One day you'll have found more treasure than you can hold and more adventure than your old bones can handle. What then?'

One day Vidar might be too old to travel, but it wouldn't be for a very long time. The answer was simple. 'When that day comes—I die. I'll die in battle and take my place in Valhalla.'

'But what if you could have a little taste of that feast in Valhalla before you go?'

Eirik had lost his reasoning somewhere along the way. Vidar shook his head. 'You're mad, Brother.

Are you trying to say that my betrothed could provide me with a taste of the pleasures to be had after my death?'

Eirik's eyes brightened and he smiled. 'That's exactly what I'm saying.'

It was Vidar's turn to laugh. 'The only pleasure that woman has in mind is the pleasure she'll have when my ballocks are served to her at her table.'

'You could change your approach,' his brother countered. 'She may want to be a warrior, but she's not. You can't win her over by defeating her.'

Vidar snorted and shook his head, walking towards his warriors on the sparring field.

'Try it, Brother,' Eirik called after him. 'A warm wife is better than a cold one.'

Vidar only shook his head again. That woman wanted to be married to him about as much as he wanted to be married to her. He'd wed her, bed her and then figure out a way to leave her behind as he went on his next adventure. They'd both be happier with that arrangement.

Chapter Five

Gwendolyn stared at the people awaiting her. They all watched her, searching her face for some reaction. A tug of humour seemed to hover around the lips of the Danes, while the Saxon faces all showed pity combined with resigned acceptance. She and Rodor had spoken to them all back in the autumn after her father had passed to explain what he'd done. They'd all had the winter to come to terms with the potential for the Danes to be invited into Alvey. And on the morning after the Danes had arrived, Rodor had gone to each and every one of the families to reassure them and reaffirm her father's word on the matter. While she was certain many of them resented the Danes, they all respected her father enough to abide by his word.

His word was still law now that he was gone. Her people would accept these Danes as allies. Gwendolyn was aware of her pivotal role in ensuring that. It was up to her to lead by example and accept her place as the wife of Vidar. Except for that morning on the sparring field, she had kept her head about her. In public she had behaved with grace and tolerance that had been acquired by never once addressing her betrothed. In private she still railed against her fate, even though she knew there was nothing to be done for it. Finally she had come to a solemn acceptance. She would marry him, but she would not submit to him.

Holding her head high, she held Annis's hand and walked across the sparring field in the light of the late afternoon. She found it ironic that they would wed on the very field of battle where they'd exchanged words just days before. Though Annis and even their parents had been married in the hall, it made more sense for Gwendolyn's wedding to take place outside so that more of their people could view their joining in marriage. Rodor had thought that having it witnessed by more people would help to ensure those same people would never have question to doubt or resent the Danes.

Gwendolyn had agreed, so she forced a smile as she made her way down the path created by the parting crowd to the centre of the group. The women had outdone themselves with the decorations. Torches were placed at intervals around the perimeter of the field to give off more light. It was early yet in the spring for flowers, so they'd hung strings of boughs and wreaths high above their heads to run between the torches. Most of the women wore crowns of ivy in their hair and Annis had even placed one over Gwendolyn's head.

Once they reached the friar Annis dropped her hand and went to stand with her husband and their two young children. Gwendolyn smiled at Rodor, but couldn't manage to keep the smile in place when she looked over at Vidar and Jarl Eirik standing beside him.

They were both handsome. Vidar's golden hair had been pulled back into a knot at the crown of his head, while his hair in the back fell in loose waves to his shoulders. Those broad shoulders were encased in a midnight-velvet tunic adorned with gold braiding and embroidery along the seams. She had to admit he had the look of a nobleman more than that of a barbarian. He also had the look of a hardened warrior, one who was accustomed to getting his way in things. It appeared allowing his wife to continue her responsibilities as they'd been before he came along wasn't part of his plan.

He was nothing like Cam. Cam had been carefree and content to allow her to do as she wanted. Vidar was the complete opposite. Intense and powerful. With Cam her life would have been calm and predictable. Nothing was predictable with this man.

His strong jaw tightened and, when he turned to look at her, his strong brow line was furrowed. She couldn't understand why he tolerated the idea of this marriage. Annis had helped her to realise that it didn't matter if he wanted it or not. If he'd called off, Jarl Eirik would have called some other man in to take his place, so it was a moot point.

His eyes widened when he took in her gown, making her realise this was the first time he'd seen her clothed in such feminine attire. Her father had brought back the velvet fabric on his last trip years ago to barter with the Scots. The sapphire colour had matched her eyes, so she'd had it made into a gown with the intention of wearing it on her wedding day, but that had been when she'd imagined Cam to be the groom. She'd almost decided against it in some sort of silent protest against the man she was forced to marry, but Annis had pointed out it would be a shame to let the gown go to waste. Gwendolyn had agreed. If she were being forced into this marriage, then at least she'd have one thing that she wanted. Well, two. She also wore her mother's favourite fox pelt stole around her shoulders to block out the chill. The amethyst necklace that Annis had gifted her completed her wedding attire.

His gaze made a sweep of her body, taking a moment to linger on her hips and the swell of her breasts. When it met hers again, she was struck by the humour shining out at her. He didn't mumble a compliment that she'd probably have seen as a pale attempt at flattery. Instead, he said, 'You honour me with your presence, my lady.'

She couldn't help it. Her lips twitched in a smile at his jest. He was baiting her, she was certain of it, but she took his bait and asked, 'Did you think I might not come?'

'I had already planned my speech to win you over.'

She did laugh then, a small giggle that she managed to stifle before it had truly escaped. The image of him pleading for her hand was so funny, she was almost sorry she hadn't made him do it. 'A pity I missed that. What did it entail? Would you have extolled my many virtues and sang a song about your many successful exploits?'

His smile widened and he took her hand. The touch was so unexpected that it wiped the smile from her lips. His fingers were strong and warm as they closed around hers, making her hand feel tiny by comparison when she had never felt tiny in her life. His skin was lightly calloused and rough against hers, but somehow the sensation wasn't repugnant. Not as it should have been.

'Not at all. I'd have promised you a say in the training of your warriors, but I must say that I'm very glad it didn't come to that.' His hand tightened around hers and he turned to face the friar, a smile still on his lips.

She followed his lead and faced the friar as well, but she ground her molars as she did so. She was almost certain he was lying, teasing her simply to make her feel that she might have got the concession from him had she only tried harder. This entire thing was a game to him and one in which only he seemed to know the rules. The friar began to speak, droning on in Latin, and she was too incensed with her groom to pay attention. She did try to jerk her hand away from him, but he only smiled wider and tucked her hand into the crook of his arm, holding it there with his other hand. Rodor gave her a disapproving look, reminding her that her people were watching and she had to put on a serene face.

So that's what she did. When it came time for her to repeat her vows, she said them loud and clear for all to hear, but she did it without once looking at her groom. Only the ceremony didn't end with the reciting of vows as it had for Annis. This one had to incorporate the Danes' own heathen tradition. Rodor had given her a quick explanation of what was to come. Now she had no choice but to participate.

As her father's only living male relative, Eadward stepped forward, bearing her father's sword in front of him. Gwendolyn took it by the hilt, her gaze lovingly tracing the carved beast's head. It was the first time she allowed herself to consider the fact that her father wasn't here to see her wed. The ache of unshed tears unexpectedly welled in her throat, forcing her to blink several times to stop them from falling. Closing her fingers around the hilt, she brought it to her chest and held it there for a moment as she said a silent prayer that she hoped would reach him.

When she opened her eyes, Vidar was facing her. His face had lost its humour. His eyes were intense and serious when they met hers. She nearly looked away from the power of his gaze, but forced herself not to. 'This sword belonged to my father. It was given to him by his father who had wielded it before him. It has held true the strength and honour of my family for generations.' Taking a deep breath, she forced the next words out. 'May it continue to do so in your hand. May it protect you and guide you as the new...' She paused and sucked in a breath, stumbling over the words. 'The new Lord of Alvey.' Holding the sword out to him, she only released the breath she'd been holding when he took it.

There. It was done. The awful thing she had dreaded was done. He was her Lord now and he'd taken her father's sword. And yet she still stood here and nothing awful had happened...yet. Perhaps their future wouldn't be so dreadful after all.

Vidar propped the sword against his leg and took the ring from the smallest finger on his left hand. She hadn't noticed it before, but it was a coiled gold band. Placing the ring on the hilt of the sword, he held it out to her, offering it to her. When she hesitated, uncertain of this ritual, he nodded and his brow raised in challenge. Swallowing thickly, she retrieved the ring. The gold would curve her finger in one complete circuit and each end was tipped with amber stone.

'With this ring, I take you as my wife. I offer you my protection and loyalty. I pledge to you that I will give my life before allowing any harm to come to yours. From now until eternity, we are one.' The

deep husk of his voice raked over her senses in a
way that she wasn't prepared to face. She'd expected
words, but somehow those words seemed genuine.
She met his gaze and saw nothing but his solemn
vow to uphold them. Her heart inexplicably beat
harder in her chest. His words didn't matter. She
knew that he'd have said those words to whomever
he'd been forced to marry, but for some reason she
didn't understand, she felt them in her heart along
with a strange awareness that fluttered in her belly.

She didn't quite know what to say. Everyone was
watching her and she realised that she should have
listened to Rodor when he'd been telling her what
to expect. As if he sensed her confusion, he stepped
forward and pressed something into her hand. It was
a ring similar to the one Vidar had given her, except
the gold was thicker. Vidar or Jarl Eirik must have
given it to Rodor, because it was clear they were a
matched set. Realising now what she was meant to
do, she balanced it on the flat of the hilt of the sword
and offered it to Vidar.

She wasn't certain what she was meant to say, so
she simply said, 'With this ring, I accept you as my
husband.' That must have done it, because he nodded and placed the ring on his finger, then he carefully wrapped his hand around the blade and took
the sword.

She'd neglected to put the ring on her finger, so
she made to rectify that, but he stopped her by covering her hand with his. Gently, he took the ring from

her and slid it on her finger. He didn't say anything, but it felt like he'd claimed her. A knot churned in her stomach. The idea of being owned by any man revolted her, but there was something about this man that terrified her.

He moved away, only to turn back with a sword Jarl Eirik had given him. It was ornate, with two rubies set into the gilded hilt. He held it out to her lying flat on both of his palms. 'I am entrusting this into your care to be given to our first-born son. May you bear me many.'

She nodded and took the sword from him, handing it off to Rodor. 'I accept,' she said, her voice low enough that only Vidar and Rodor were likely to hear her. 'But we never agreed to children.'

Now that the ceremony was finished, he'd relaxed and even smiled at her when she said that. 'I'm looking forward to the challenge, my lady.'

He didn't seem fazed at all, or even worried that he wouldn't be able to win the challenge. She frowned and her scowl deepened when the Danes gave up a mighty cheer when Vidar took her hand and raised it.

They were well and truly wed now.

Vidar brought her hand to his lips, but his gaze caught on her full lips. They were soft and pink and he longed to kiss them. From the moment she had appeared in her gown, he'd been struck by this fierce wave of possessiveness. It was as if his body hadn't recognised her as his until that very moment, which made no sense because she'd been his since the first moment he'd seen her.

Perhaps it was that she hadn't seemed quite so feminine then. Nay, that wasn't right, because even now he could recall how her hips and buttocks had appeared very womanly in the glimpse he'd had beneath her long tunic. Then he realised what it was. It wasn't the gown, though the deep blue colour complimented her greatly. It wasn't that her hair had been left to fall down her back beneath the veil.

It was her eyes. She looked for all the world like a queen as she looked at him. Her chin was raised proudly as if she challenged him to touch her. But beneath that exterior, her eyes were vulnerable. There was a crack in her façade and she was terrified. Whether she realised it or not, he couldn't say, but she was looking to him for reassurance.

That thought sobered him and he was struck with how much power he held over her. Never in his life, never once—including his many battles and their casualties—had he had such control over the life of one person. Or more specifically the livelihood and contentment of one person. As she stared down at him, her eyes revealing more vulnerability than she knew, he became drunk on that power. Began to revel in it, even. She was beautiful and strong. A veritable queen.

And she was his.

Their cheering grew louder as his men came up

behind him. Before he realised what they meant to do, they'd hoisted him over their shoulders to carry him off to celebrate. A marriage was always something to celebrate, whether the couple were happy with the arrangement or not.

'Congratulations, Brother!' Eirik called out as he took a place under Vidar's right side, his arms wrapped around Vidar's thigh. 'You'll do Alvey proud.'

Vidar smiled as he looked out over Alvey and its people. The Danes were celebrating and, drawn by the allure, some of the Saxons were starting to join in. The gates were open to the people of the countryside and many of them had turned out, curious to the festivities. Several large fires had been going since midday and the air was heavy with the scent of roasting lamb and venison mingled with spices he couldn't identify.

The place seemed well fortified, self-sufficient and profitable. Surprisingly, he did feel a swell of pride. Alvey was his. If she was these people's queen, then he was their king. Many of them even bowed their heads in deference as his men strode by, intent on making a complete circle of the grounds within the wall. He could become accustomed to this.

Night had fallen completely by the time the men led him to the open door of the hall. Servants moved in and out, carrying platters of food inside to those

who'd been lucky enough to be invited in to celebrate with the bride and groom. A cheer went up
when Vidar stepped inside and Rolfe clapped him
on the back as he went off to find a spot at one of
the crowded tables. There was no question where
Vidar would sit. Gwendolyn's usual chair had been
replaced with a high-backed bench wide enough to
accommodate him.

Eirik and Rodor had already taken their seats and
seemed to be telling each other stories of past battles. Vidar barely spared them any attention. Gwendolyn held his gaze and he couldn't look away from
her. She'd taken off her veil, so her dark hair flowed
in loose waves around her shoulders. It was a star-
tling contrast to her pale skin and her wide blue
eyes shone in the firelight like jewels. She really
was breathtaking. He wasn't sure how he'd missed
that when he'd first seen her.

Pride swelled in his chest as he walked towards
her, much like something else swelled in his trousers. He glanced at the men who called out to him
from across the room to make it go away, while
being thankful his tunic covered him. Giving them a
nod and a wave, he made his way through the crowd
and approached her.

His wife. The word stumbled through his brain
before finding traction. It didn't seem the profanity
that it had before.

'Good evening, Wife.' He smiled at the startled

look she gave him. Her eyes widened beneath the dark fringe of her lashes.

'There's no need to gloat,' she said and turned back to watching the servants as they placed platters of food on the table before them.

He smiled as he took his place beside her, already enjoying their verbal sparring sessions. As he settled in, he realised that he'd never sat this close to her before. His leg stretched out and his thigh pressed against the length of hers. She shifted, but there wasn't very much room on the bench with them both occupying it. The heat from her body penetrated the layers of their clothes and he found himself warming to her, his skin prickling from her closeness.

'Is it gloating to call you my wife?' Through the smells of the food, he detected her own sweet scent. Taking a deep breath, he turned his head slightly and realised that it was her hair. He couldn't pinpoint what the scent was, but he liked it very much. It was soft and infinitely feminine.

'I'm not certain how you Danes spar, but here it's considered unsportsmanlike to gloat over a victory in front of the loser.' She kept her gaze on the table, nodding at a servant who offered her a pitcher of ale.

Vidar laughed. 'That's the most ridiculous thing I've ever heard. Why would a victor not be allowed to celebrate his win?' Then he grabbed her empty goblet just as the servant woman was about to fill it with ale.

That earned him a glare from his wife. 'Because

everyone knows he won. There's no need to rub it in the fallen opponent's face.' She made a grab for the goblet, but Vidar held it back out of her reach. 'It only leads to bad feelings.'

'Ah, you mean it only leads to bad feelings for the fallen. If that's the case, then that's a weakness for the fallen one to overcome, wouldn't you say? It's no fault of the victorious winner.'

She grabbed for the goblet again, nearly coming to her feet to reach across him for it. Vidar inhaled, filling his nose with that sweet scent, and the soft swell of her breasts brushed against his chest. All the blood in his body rushed to his groin. By the gods, he looked forward to claiming her later that night.

'Of course you'd see it that way,' she said and sat back down. Giving up on trying to reclaim her goblet, she asked for the servant to bring another.

To her credit, the woman looked to him for confirmation. He shook his head and the woman stood immobile, uncertain whose displeasure she should incur. Vidar took pity on her and explained his intention. 'We have no need of ale this night or any night for the next month.' The woman's brow furrowed in confusion but she nodded and said, 'Aye, my lord', before moving down the table.

When his bride raised a questioning brow, Vidar also decided to put her out of her misery. Apparently weddings made him feel generous, he mused. 'Tradition calls for us to share a cask of specially made mead on our wedding night and every night after until it's gone.'

'Ah, well, unfortunately we didn't know and haven't prepared such a cask for the occasion.'

'Doesn't matter. My brother brought one for us.'

She frowned and he bit back a smile. Raising his hand, he signalled for Rolfe. Rolfe let out a cheer and the men around him followed suit as he made his way to the corner where the cask had been left earlier in the day. Hefting it over his shoulder, he brought it over to a stool that someone rushed to put next to Vidar.

Vidar rose and took the hammer and chisel someone shoved into his hands. In a moment he broke the seal on the cask and lifted the lid. Rolfe handed him the large tankard made of gold and encrusted with a row of tiny rubies along the bottom edge. It had come from Eirik's home and was the same one he and Merewyn had used after their marriage. Filling the cup, he raised it high in the air. 'I drink to my new bride and the success of our marriage. May our union prove fruitful with many sons and daughters.' He repeated the words in his own language so that even the ones who didn't fully comprehend the Saxon tongue could understand. Then he stared at Gwendolyn as he brought the cup to his lips to drink.

She stared back, clearly rattled by his words. Had she truly thought that she'd be allowed to participate in the marriage without the prospect of children? If nothing else, they needed to have children to ensure the survival of the Alvey line, not to mention his own lineage.

Swallowing, he lowered the cup and offered her a sip, bringing the cup to her lips. Her eyes flashed with defiance, but he'd already seen her display of loyalty to her people at the wedding. She wouldn't give them reason to dispute the marriage by denying him now. She brought her hands to the goblet, but he didn't relinquish it to her. He held it and tipped it gently so that she could drink from him.

Again, the power of his control over her nearly overwhelmed him with pleasure. She was strong and wilful, but he found the small glimpses of obedience he had from her were very satisfying. So satisfying that he decided to press his advantage. The men cheered this ceremonial display of their joining, but he couldn't resist pushing it further. Dropping down to sit beside her, he placed the goblet on the table and then turned to her. Her eyes widened as she speculated his intent, but he didn't make her wait long as he put one hand behind her, burying his fingers in her thick hair, and his other hand on her hip to draw her close. Without waiting for her compliance, he tilted her head back and covered her mouth with his.

The sweet taste of the honeyed mead greeted his lips. When she gasped in shock, he took advantage and dipped the tip of his tongue inside, greedy for more of her sweetness. But he was no fool. She was too fierce to allow him such liberties, so he drew back from her before she could push him away.

His gaze met hers and he was right that she was angry, but her eyes shone with curiosity, as well. Her gaze focused on his mouth and the tip of her tongue ran across her own bottom lip before she put a hand to her mouth. She looked away and the cheers from his men became louder. A few of them made crude remarks about the night to come and her face reddened.

He gave the perpetrators a sharp glare that effectively silenced them. Aye, he was the victor in this battle, but he wasn't naïve enough to believe he wouldn't face an uphill battle with her. He hadn't intended to humiliate her in front of his men. He'd intended to stake his claim to her publicly.

She was his wife. She would be his wife in all ways before the night was over.

The Viking Warrior's Bride

Chapter Six

Gwendolyn struggled to keep her eyes open as she waited for the storyteller to finish his tale. She'd have left for her chamber while everyone was captivated by his story of her husband's bravery across the sea, but she knew that would have offended the man and reflected badly on his craft. It wasn't his fault she wasn't particularly impressed with his obviously embellished story. When he claimed that Vidar had defeated a sea monster the size of two ships, she rolled her eyes. When he went on to declare that Vidar had taken on twenty men with only his sword, she snorted her disbelief, drawing the gaze of her offended husband.

Propping an elbow on the bench's high back, he leaned over and kept his voice low to ask, 'You don't believe I fought twenty men?'

His breath caressed her ear in a way that left her skin tingling, so she shifted away from him a little. It seemed that she had spent the entire night shifting away from him to no avail. The bench wasn't wide enough to leave much space between them. She couldn't help but think that the bench's maker had somehow conspired against her. 'Not by yourself.'

He grinned down at her and his gaze narrowed in on her mouth as if remembering how he'd kissed her hours before. 'But you've never seen me fight.'

'Don't have to. You forget, I know about swords.'

He didn't speak for a moment and their attention moved back to the storyteller. Vidar's hand rested on her shoulder and his thumb began to stroke a small circle on the velvet of her gown. Every now and then the rough tip would graze her neck, making her skin prickle in pleasure. 'But you've never seen *my* sword,' he finally said.

Something about that gave her pause. She dared to shift her gaze to his and he was looking at her again, his eyes rather predatory this time as he teased her. She was almost entirely certain that they weren't talking about swords any more. 'I believe all swords work the same.'

He shrugged. 'Some are smaller than others. Some broader and heavier. Would you like to know what mine is like?'

She swallowed as her mouth went dry. She was entirely certain now that he was not speaking of swords. She was even more certain that she was as curious as she was terrified about his...um, sword.

'It's longer than most and a bit thicker, I'm told—'

She stood up, knocking his hand off her shoulder and probably interrupting those around her who seemed interested in the lies the storyteller was telling, but she refused to sit and listen to Vidar prattle on about his *sword* any longer. He was smiling as she nudged past him and slowly got to his feet to allow her to pass.

'Are you retiring for the evening, my lady?' Jarl Eirik rose to his feet.

'Aye, it's been a long day and I'm very tired.'

He gave Vidar a questioning look, as if he suspected he was the cause of her leaving early, but her husband merely shrugged. 'I'll give you some time alone,' Vidar generously offered.

She resisted the urge to remind him that they wouldn't be consummating the marriage, but decided that it was best to save that conversation for when they had privacy. Instead, she ignored him and made her way to the stone stairway at the back of the hall. Annis, who'd been seated at the table next to Jarl Eirik, followed her. The stairs made a turn, creating a short hallway lit by a torch that revealed the single door at the top. The master's chamber was secluded here and much safer for it. Gwendolyn didn't much like having to share the room with him, but she understood that everyone expected it. She'd decided that she'd be cordial and allow him to share it with her as long as he didn't touch her.

'He seems much nicer than you let on,' Annis said as she closed the door behind them, her brow creased.

Gwendolyn snorted and reached for the ties on her garment. 'He's not nice at all.' Annis hurried over and helped her out of the gown, taking it over to the corner of the room where she draped it over a chest to be brushed in the morning before it was put away.

'Well he's certainly not cruel, nor is he offensive. He's actually very handsome.'

Gwendolyn gave another snort as she tossed the linen nightrail over her head.

'You can't say he doesn't cut a fine figure,' Annis argued.

No, she couldn't say that. Despite her best effort to hate the man, Gwendolyn could admit to herself that she found him attractive. Putting her hands through the arms of the nightrail, she smoothed the bleached linen down her body. 'I never said that I didn't find him attractive. But it takes more than a fine face to be a good leader and warrior.' It was true. 'Cam wasn't particularly attractive, as those things go, but I respected him far more than this man.'

It bothered her that she hadn't thought of Cam very much over the past few days. Particularly not today. He'd been the man she'd been set on marrying since she'd been a girl, yet he had barely crossed her thoughts as she'd been pledging herself to that barbarian.

'Cam was a good man.' Annis took her hand and led her over to the stool set before the round of polished silver where she kept her comb. Pushing her down to sit, Annis picked up the comb and worked through Gwendolyn's hair, her brow still furrowed in concern. 'Gwendolyn, I feel I've been remiss in my duty to you. I've never properly explained what you should expect tonight and I should've told you much earlier so you could prepare.'

Her stomach twisted and she swallowed against the lump of guilt that had wedged in her throat. 'Annis...it's not necessary, believe me.'

'Nay, it is necessary. I should've told you.'

Turning on the stool, Gwendolyn took her sister's hand to stop her from combing her hair. 'It's not. You see, I know what will happen.'

Annis's brow furrowed, but then as realisation dawned, her eyes widened in shock. 'Gwendolyn! How do you know? What's happened?'

Gwendolyn closed her eyes against the censure on her sister's face. 'It was the night before Cam was leaving for battle. I went to him to tell him goodbye and it just happened. I didn't think much of it at the time, because I thought that he'd be coming home and we'd be married soon after.' Though she'd cared for Cam very much, the actual act hadn't left her feeling particularly thrilled about repeating it. She'd been happy that he seemed to have found so much pleasure in the act. Had Cam returned home, she'd have lain with him again and again to give him that happiness.

It was not something that she wanted to share with Vidar.

'But you weren't wed, Gwendolyn.'

'I know, but it doesn't matter. It was nigh on two years ago. And I thought we would be married soon or I wouldn't have done it.'

Annis let out a disappointed breath. 'Well, I suppose it doesn't matter now. At least you know what to expect.'

'Oh, I won't be lying with that barbarian.'

Her sister sucked in a harsh breath. 'Your husband? You won't lie with your husband?' she whispered, as if the idea was wicked.

Gwendolyn shook her head. 'He married me for Alvey. He'll have Alvey, but that doesn't mean he'll have my body.'

Annis didn't say anything as she resumed brushing Gwendolyn's hair, but Gwendolyn could tell that her sister had been scandalised. For some reason, unwelcome guilt began to eat at her and that was swiftly followed by anger. It wasn't her fault she'd been forced into this.

'You disapprove,' she said quietly.

'Nay, I don't disapprove.' Annis combed through a particularly bad tangle and Gwendolyn winced. 'You did not ask for this marriage, and I can't even begin to imagine how it must feel to be expected to lie with a man you don't even know. I'd known Eadward for my whole life before we wed.' She sat the comb down on the table and worked the knot with her fingers. 'However, I do feel that you're not even giving this marriage a chance. I want you to have what Eadward and I share and I know that might sound naïve…you might never have that with Vidar. We don't even know him. But I do feel that you can have a cordial relationship. One that is based on mutual respect and a belief in doing what is best for Alvey and our people.'

'But I do want what is best for Alvey. Did you not see me marry Vidar? Did you not see that I didn't stomp and wail as I wanted to do?'

Finished with the knot, Annis smoothed her palm down Gwendolyn's back and nodded. 'Aye, I saw that. You followed Father's wishes and did what was best for us. Now I'm asking that you do what is best for you. Try to find a way to work with your husband.' Taking Gwendolyn's face in her hands, Annis kissed her on each cheek. 'I have to go. Goodnight, sweet sister. I'll see you in the morning, but I'm leaving with Eadward and the children after the morning meal.'

Gwendolyn wished her sister a good sleep and watched her leave, feeling very much as if the only person she could count on was abandoning her. With a sigh, Gwendolyn rose to her feet and grabbed her dressing gown from the peg on the wall. Slipping into it, she wrapped the thick garment around her and went to bed, leaving a few candles burning so that Vidar wouldn't stumble over anything in the dark. And that was as far as she was willing to go with affection on her wedding night.

Vidar had watched his wife's departure from the feast with more interest than he would have thought possible when he'd arrived at Alvey three days ago. He'd never wanted this marriage and if he'd had his choice then he'd still be fighting in the south, but now that she was his, he was liking the idea more and more. There was no question that he was attracted to her. The only question now was how long before she'd admit to the mutual attraction he'd seen flickering in her eyes when he'd kissed her. The woman had her pride, so he had no doubt that she'd continue to fight it.

He'd turned his attention back to the storyteller who'd started in on another tale, this one featuring Eirik, when the subtle cheers from the back of the large room drew his attention. Some of the younger warriors had pushed their way back there, perched at the bottom of the steps to wait for either Gwendolyn or her sister to re-emerge from the master's chamber. Annis had stoked their shouts with her descent down the stairs.

Eirik leaned over and said with a grin, 'You should go join your wife before they get louder. I believe she already plans to challenge you this evening. You don't want those dolts making her angrier.'

Vidar nodded and got to his feet. Eirik was right. If those cheers went on for long and reached her ears, then she'd not only be angry but offended. Best to go now while the battle could still be controlled. Unfortunately, the cheers seemed to gain in volume the closer he walked to the steps, even drowning out the storyteller so the man stopped talking altogether. Some of his men had taken offence to her challenging him on the sparring field and he suspected that this was their way of seeing her get her comeuppance.

He was unprepared, however, when Rolfe walked up beside him. 'Let's deliver the man to his wife!' his friend yelled. Before Vidar realised what was happening, Rolfe along with someone else, hoisted him on to their shoulders. A few more men joined in until there seemed to be a wave of warriors delivering him to Gwendolyn's bed.

'Release me,' he yelled, but his voice was drowned out by the cheers and his own laughter. He knew a moment of fear when the drunken horde carried him up the stairs and they wobbled near the top, but someone kicked the door open and the entire group, which had grown to at least a score of men, fell inside. Thankfully, Rolfe and the one who held Vidar's other leg, kept their feet, but only barely. They stumbled over the fallen men, barely making it to the bed before dropping him next to his very startled wife.

Gwendolyn sat there, her eyes wide in fear and the blanket drawn up to her neck. That fear quickly gave way to anger when she realised no one was there to maul her and she narrowed her eyes at him. He pre-emptively turned back to his warriors. 'Out!' he yelled and got to his feet. A few of them heeded his words, but the others still sat around. 'Out.'

'Isn't there some law about needing to verify the union?' one of them said.

'Get out of this chamber or, by the Gods, I'll throw you down the stairs.' Vidar walked towards the man, but he scrambled to his feet and fled.

Rolfe laughed and clapped Vidar on the back as he left. 'Remember, patience. I know it's not your strength, but the women appreciate it.'

Vidar bit out a harsh curse and pushed him out the door. Rolfe's laughter floated back to him and the last man had barely escaped before Vidar slammed the thick door behind them. He took a deep breath before he turned to face his wife, already knowing what he would find waiting for him. 'That was not my idea,' he said, pointing towards the door.

'It wasn't your idea to arrive on the backs of your warriors like some conquering barbarian? How surprising.' She'd settled back against her pillows and had loosened her death grip on the blanket.

He swallowed, determined to not call out her unfair treatment of him. After all, the warrior in him understood it. He'd feel the same if he'd lost in battle and the victor were delivered to him in the same manner. But he hadn't come to gloat. He'd come to claim what was rightfully his and what she was obligated to give him.

Unquestionable claim to Alvey from all who might challenge him.

Ignoring her rancour, he strode to his chest which had been placed at the foot of the bed earlier that day. Vidar hadn't actually seen the chamber himself, so he took a look around as he sat down on the chest and started taking off his boots. The chamber was larger than he'd expected. The ceiling was much lower than the one in the great room downstairs and the stone walls were draped in thick tapestries to keep in the heat from the small hearth in the corner. A slat in the stonework above it gave the smoke a place to reach the outside. A high chest stood along one wall, along with shelves along the far wall that held scrolls and a knife collection that he'd have to examine in the morning.

As he tossed his boots to the side, he turned his attention to the bed. It was a rather elaborate affair with a curving headboard made of wood and four posts draped with fabric to keep in the warmth. An image of his wife in that bed with the dark fabric contrasting against her pale skin came to mind and he couldn't get it to leave. She looked more welcoming in his mind than she did at the moment, however. Her cheeks were flushed, but it was in anger and not arousal.

He nearly sighed aloud at the task ahead. He'd never had to stoop to seducing a woman in his life. From the time he'd first found interest in the female form, there'd been many eager to keep him company. Some of it was because he'd had a reputation for being generous to the women he sought to warm his bed, but he wasn't bad to look upon. He'd been solicited many times when he'd been in a new place and his wealth hadn't been known. Never once had a woman looked upon him with the open disgust evident on his wife's face.

Shrugging out of his tunic and his undershirt, he laid them both across the chest.

'What are you doing?' she asked, her grip tightening on the blanket again.

'Coming to bed,' he explained. Walking around to pull the blanket back on his side of the bed, he blew out the candle on the small table there. A candle still flickered on the table set up with her toiletries, so he thought it best to proceed slowly. She looked ready to bolt and the last thing he wanted was to frighten her unnecessarily by taking his trousers off and setting her off.

She exhaled in what could only be relief and relaxed into her pillow.

He laid there next to her, uncertain for the first time in his life on how to proceed with a woman. To be fair, while he found her attractive, having required relations with her wasn't high on the list of things he wanted to do that night. Though, if the rise in his trousers was any indication, his body was up for the task.

'Gwendolyn—'

'You've won my hand,' she began at the same time. 'Let that be enough.'

Vidar frowned and rolled over to look at her. 'What do you mean?'

Her wide-eyed gaze met his. 'It means that we do not need to take this further.'

'Further? You mean consummation?'

She nodded. 'Of course that's what I mean.'

Vidar took in a deep breath, certain now that he understood her hesitation. If he were in her shoes, he'd probably feel the same. He couldn't imagine being forced to lie with someone he didn't want. Then he nearly laughed because that was exactly what was happening, only in his case, a part of him did want her very much. He wanted this brave and strong woman beneath him, crying out his name in pleasure as he drove into her over and over again. He wanted her clinging to his shoulders, her nails scraping down his back as he made her come apart. And that quickly, his erection was at full attention. He reached down and shifted his trousers to find a more comfortable position.

'You're my wife now, Gwendolyn, and I'm your husband. In all ways I will protect you and keep you safe. Even in this.' He reached out to touch the back of her hand with his fingertips.

She sucked in a shaky breath and looked down at the contact before looking back at him. The way her eyes widened and her breathing increased made him think she actually did enjoy his touch very much. He refused to rub that knowledge in and tucked it away to revel in later.

'I'll go slowly and there are ways to prepare

you. It may hurt at first, but you will learn to find pleasure—'

She moved so fast he barely had a chance to drop his hand before she'd reached beneath the stack of pillows and pulled out a knife. Its jewelled hilt matched the ones he'd seen on the shelf.

'Let me say this very clearly so you'll understand. We will not be consummating this marriage.' She emphasised each word in the statement.

'You've gone daft.'

She smiled, revealing an even row of teeth. 'You remember that next time you try to touch me and you'll keep your fingers intact.'

Vidar stared at her, completely taken off guard by her refusal. He knew she'd battle him, but he never imagined that she'd completely deny him what was his by right. The woman was as brazen as they came and he'd have to tame her before it was all over.

Getting to his feet beside the bed, he yanked at the fastenings of his trousers. She narrowed her eyes at him and tightened her grip on the knife pointed at him.

'What the blazes are you doing?' she asked.

Tossing his trousers to land in a heap on his clothes at the end of the bed, he said, 'Going to bed. Do not worry.' He got back into bed nude and pulled the blanket up over him. 'I won't force myself on you. Your surrender will be all the sweeter when it's given willingly.' With that he turned his back on her and hoped he didn't awake with that dagger shoved into it.

Chapter Seven

Gwendolyn stared into the light of the single candle that flickered across the room. Vidar was snoring softly at her side, but she'd yet to be able to fall asleep. Despite her best efforts, every time she closed her eyes she saw his nude body. He'd been as strong and wrapped in muscle as she'd thought he might be. His tunics had hinted at the broad shoulders, thick chest and strong arms beneath, but the hint had been a mere shadow of the real thing.

And though she'd spent most of her life around men and warriors and had thought herself immune to the pleasures of their physiques, something about *his* made her cheeks warm and a tingle of something unrecognisable zing through her belly. The knife safely tucked beneath her pillow, she brought her hands to her cheeks in an effort to cool them off. She made the mistake of closing her eyes and there he was again. An image of his golden strength and masculinity seared through her mind. Even his thighs had been thick with muscle. And that man part of his…

She forced her eyes open so she wouldn't dwell on it, but she couldn't stop. It, too, had been strong and thick and, for some reason she couldn't begin to fathom, she was curious about it. An ache had begun between her thighs, causing her to squeeze them together to assuage it. What was wrong with her? She didn't like this man in the least, but her body was certainly curious about him. Holding the blanket tight against her, she rolled over very slowly so that she wouldn't wake him. His breathing continued to be deep and even, so she took a moment to study him closer.

In sleep, his expression lost the fierceness and the almost smug quality that she had come to associate with him. The grooves around his mouth had softened enough for her to realise that he really had beautifully proportioned lips. The bottom lip was slightly fuller than the top and they were curved in a slight bow. She tried to remember Cam's lips, but she couldn't and that made her feel terrible. To be fair, she'd never spent a great deal of time looking at Cam. He'd been supportive of her archery skills, and had been a very good friend of her brother's, so his appearance hadn't been something that she'd considered very much.

Flopping on to her back, she did her best to recreate his image. He hadn't been golden like the Dane next to her. His hair and eyes had been dark. The women in the hall didn't stop and stare at him, like she'd noticed they did with Vidar, but neither had Cam been unattractive. He'd always just been Cam.

But he'd been kind. She'd take a kind and easy-going Cam over this infuriating outsider any day. It would take more than a handsome face and pleasing body to sway her. She would make sure of it.

Closing her eyes again, she forced herself to calm down and finally managed to drift off to sleep.

When she opened her eyes again, it was much later because the candle had burned out and the room was black as pitch. She wasn't certain what had awakened her, but her heart pounded in her chest and her breath came fast and hard like it did when she was sparring. Only, the sound of her breath wasn't the only sound she heard. His harsh breath had joined hers. It brushed against her ear, causing her skin to prickle.

'Gwendolyn,' he whispered as he placed his lovely mouth against her neck.

She shivered and realised why her heart was pounding so hard. His hand had found its way up her nightdress and was cupping the mound between her thighs. 'Vidar.' She stiffened and grabbed his arm, her fingers squeezing the hard muscle that flexed beneath him, but she couldn't bring herself to push him away. Her body was aching—*throbbing*—for his touch. She didn't know what was happening, but somehow she knew that his fingers would make it stop.

'Open your legs for me,' he whispered, taking the lobe of her ear between his teeth. His fingertips caressed the down at the apex of her thighs.

His command was so wicked and unexpected that she opened her mouth to say nay, but she didn't really want to deny him. She wanted to know what he would do if she followed his command. Taking her lip between her teeth, she raised her knee just a little, pushing it out to the side. Somehow it seemed all right to allow this experiment to go on. After all, it was dark and the blanket still covered them.

His long fingers moved down between her lips, finding her centre. He groaned harshly against her ear as his two middle fingers moved up and down spreading the wetness she was surprised to feel there. 'Ah, you're so wet.'

She blushed, unsure exactly what was happening—was being wet a good thing or something about which to be embarrassed?—and tightened her thighs. But it was too late to hold him back, because the tip of his longest finger had already dipped inside her. Where she ached the most. The source of the slick heat.

She gasped and bit down on her lip to stifle the sound. He laughed softy against her neck, the sound both approval and a gentle taunting. He dragged the broad tip of his finger up over her sex to the nub at the top, bringing that wetness with him. Her flesh

was so sensitive that she jumped at the contact, but
he soothed her with a kiss as he nuzzled her neck.
Then his finger made a circle around that spot, moving slowly over and over again until her hips were
chasing him. When he tired of that, he dragged it
over the swollen flesh, setting off a flare of lights
behind her eyelids. Then it didn't matter that he was
Vidar or that this was probably wicked in some way
she couldn't even fathom, it only mattered that he
continued to touch her.

'Are you ready?' His finger continued to stroke
her, but he raised up enough that she felt his breath
against her cheek, though she still couldn't see his
face in the pitch darkness. 'I want to be inside you.'
He spoke the words, but his voice held a note of request. He was asking permission, and that alone,
perhaps even more than his touch, made her want
him to.

'Aye,' she said. Her body throbbed for his possession and her hand, which had lain dormant at her
side all this time, reached up to touch that which was
so close. He was hard and long and she wrapped
her fingers around him, marvelling at his thickness.
When he groaned in obvious pleasure, she squeezed
simply to wring the sound from his lips again.

'I need you.' His voice was husky with need and
he leaned in and whispered filthy words about just
what part of her he needed. When she let him go,
he climbed over her, pushing her knees apart with
his heavy thighs.

She held her breath, waiting for his invasion, knowing that it would counter the throbbing. Her hips pushed against him and her leg curled around his hip, but no matter how she moved, he wouldn't come inside her. He moved back away from her and she grabbed at him to no avail. He slipped out of her hands.

'Vidar,' she gasped. 'Nay, come back.' She made a grab for him and her eyes flew open.

Her body still throbbed, but his hand wasn't between her thighs. It wasn't even pitch dark. Faint morning light filtered in through the vent slats beneath the roof. The skirt of her nightgown had ridden up past her knees and she was so warm, she'd tossed the blanket off her legs. Bringing her hand to her chest, she covered her pounding heart. Part of her wondered if the dream had been real, while the other wondered how she'd had such a provocative dream. He'd touched her in a way that no one ever had. If it had been a dream, how had she even known to conjure it up? Her one time with Cam had been fast and perfunctory in the woods beside the river. There'd been no touching, at least not like that.

Anger threatened to swell within her, but she was too confused to give it free rein. She tried to turn to see if he was still there and awake, but then she realised why she was so hot. He was pressed up against her back, overheating her. His breath rustled her hair and his chest brushed her back as he breathed in. His hands weren't on her, though. If he had actually touched her so intimately, his hand would still be on her, wouldn't it?

She turned her head a bit to look at him over her shoulder and saw that his eyes were closed. He was sleeping. She shifted to slide off the bed, hoping to leave the room before he awoke, but she stilled when something hard nudged her hip. Her face flamed and her heart thundered. He was erect. That male part of him was just as hard as it had been last night.

Her body's response was immediate. Heat flooded her centre and the delicious ache she hoped she'd left behind in her dream returned. She wanted him. She'd dreamed about him in the night and she wanted him now that it was morning. What was happening to her?

She slid away, but his hand moved to grab her hip, holding her in place.

'Good morning, wife.' His voice was rough with morning huskiness as he leaned forward and took a deep breath. 'Your hair smells good.'

Something about his words or the sound of his voice made her nipples tighten and a tendril of excitement curl through her belly. If she closed her eyes, she could almost pretend that they were a true husband and wife waking up with the morning. But she would not close her eyes and pretend any such thing. Disturbing things happened to her when she closed her eyes so close to him. 'Good morning,' she whispered.

Gently and with a subtlety she'd have thought beneath him, he pulled her hip back so that her bottom was pressed against his male appendage. Her gown and nightrail were between them, but she could still feel that he was hot and possibly throbbing, but she wasn't sure if she'd imagined that part. Her own body was throbbing and she could barely feel anything beyond that.

He nuzzled her neck, his nose dragging a path upward towards her ear. The soft scrape of his beard left a pleasant tingle in its wake. She sucked in a breath when he pushed his hips against her, allowing her to feel how hard and thick he was. For her. She nearly groaned aloud as an answering swell of arousal moved through her.

'Have you reconsidered your refusal to allow me to properly bed you?'

Ice water couldn't have done a better job at squelching her arousal for him. 'This is all a game for you, isn't it? See how quickly you can get me to capitulate to you?' She tugged away from him, gaining her feet beside the bed and wrapping her thick nightrail around her.

He grinned at her and rolled on to his back, bringing his hands up to rest beneath his head. He didn't even bother to hide his erection with the blanket. 'I do enjoy games. But I woke up with a soft and very aroused woman beside me. I merely thought that bedding you would be a good way to pass the morning.'

'I was not aroused.' Even as she blatantly denied the truth, her face flamed and his smile only widened.

His gaze dropped to the apex of her thighs. 'Do not deny that you are slick with wanting me.'

'I knew it.' She tightened the nightrail around her even though she knew that he couldn't see anything. 'You were touching me while I slept. It wasn't a dream. How dare you touch me without my permission!'

The look of shock that came over his face and dropped his chin to his chest could not have been faked. His smile had completely vanished in the wake of his surprise. He had no idea what she was talking about. 'You dreamed that I touched you?'

Oh, dear God, what power had she given him over her? She swallowed thickly and floundered in the weight of her revelation. 'Nay... I don't... You...'

Despite the fact that he might have gloated and teased her, his face sobered and he said, 'I would never force my attention on you. I knew you were slick because I could smell your arousal.' She gasped. Both at his bravado in saying such a wicked thing out loud and because she had no idea if such a thing were possible. But he wasn't finished. 'When I do take you—and I *will* take you—it will be with your full submission to me.'

He was so certain of himself that she was struck speechless. That is, until he reached for his male part with his right hand. It stood up proudly, reaching for his navel, not in the least subdued by their minor skirmish. 'What are you doing?'

His hand paused halfway to its goal. 'I'm taking care of what you started…unless you'd like to do it.'

'What? Nay! I will not submit to you. I will not bed you.'

He shrugged one shoulder. 'How about just using your mouth then? We won't call it a full submission.'

Her mouth? She couldn't fathom if such a thing were even possible or if he was simply taunting her. Either way, he was mad if he thought she'd touch him with any part of her body. 'I'd rather suck on a rotten eel.'

Shrugging again, he said, 'Then I suppose I have no choice but to take care of this myself.' Then he took himself in hand and closed his eyes as he laid his head back on the pillow. 'You can watch if it interests you.'

She turned away as his fingers wrapped around the thing, his thumb moving over the broad head. 'You vulgar… Dane.' There was no curse word offensive enough to describe him. 'I cannot believe my father forced me to marry someone such as you.'

His response was a low moan of pleasure as his hand worked up and down his shaft. Her face burning in anger and a strange feeling she couldn't bear to call arousal, she hurried from the chamber intent on finding Rodor and forcing…nay, begging him to banish the rude man from her bed.

Chapter Eight

The crisp morning air wasn't enough to put a damper on Vidar's *interest* in his wife. But if a few moments in bed working to assuage the need on his own hadn't tempered it, then the air didn't stand a chance. Nevertheless, he turned his face into the cool wind and gave it a try.

Nay. Damn the bloody woman, he was still half-rigid in his trousers. The memory of waking up to her lush bottom pressed against his hard flesh refused to leave him. He'd imagined gently pushing her forward and sliding into her from behind. It would have been slow and easy and so bloody satisfying they'd have wanted to do it all morning. His hand had been a poor substitute for her sweet passage gripping him tight as he'd made them both feel good. It was no wonder that his body wasn't satisfied.

With an exhale of frustration, he walked towards the sparring field. He had hope that he'd be able to crack her defences by the end of a sennight together. He hadn't been lying when he'd told her that he'd known she was aroused. Her need had been on her face and he'd plainly seen the hard points of her nipples beading beneath her clothes. Perhaps she couldn't even admit that to herself, but she wanted him. Mutual attraction sparked between them whenever he was near her and he knew it wasn't just one sided. The fact that she had dreamed about him only proved it. He had a feeling that his wife wasn't nearly as prudish as she tried to let on. He wouldn't rest until he'd drawn out every one of her hidden desires.

'Morning,' Rolfe said from where he lounged against the wall of the armoury, his gaze across the sparring field.

It shouldn't have come as a surprise to see his wife out on the field, back in her trousers and tunic today, leading her men through a sparring session. She'd been absent at the morning meal and he might have guessed she'd try to beat him out here. Nevertheless, Vidar sighed to release his frustration as he watched. 'What is she doing?'

Rolfe shrugged. 'They were out there when I got here.' Several of his men were lounging around the field, watching Gwendolyn as she led her warriors in sparring practice. They weren't using the blocked-out pattern that he'd been teaching them. This was shaping up to be a repeat of his first morning here.

Nodding, Vidar took off across the field, gaining the notice of many of her men who faltered in their movements. She glanced over her shoulder and frowned when she noticed him. 'What do you want?' she asked.

'I need the field to train.' He wanted to tell her that she was overstepping her bounds, but was attempting to keep their discourse civil.

'Then you'll need to wait or find another place.'

Gritting his teeth at her attempt to waylay him, he stifled the urge to call her out on her defiance. She was bent on pushing him to the edge of his tolerance. 'Perhaps we can discuss a schedule.' He bit the words out.

'Perhaps we can. Later.' Then she turned her back on him.

He nearly growled in frustration and touched her arm to turn her back around. She had no business interfering in his work. She had no place on the sparring field. But to tell her that would only make things worse and another idea struck him as he opened his mouth. His wife had already proven that she wasn't very good at obeying commands. So he wouldn't give her one. Instead, he said, 'I challenge you to a tournament.'

She blinked, her face a blank mask as she sensed the trap that she couldn't see. 'What sort of tournament?'

'Five of my best men against five of yours. They'll fight with weapons and then without. And we will see who has the better warriors.'

Her eyes narrowed on him, still suspicious. 'Why would you want to do that?'

He crossed his arms over his chest. 'Because if you lose, you agree to give up control of training the men to me.'

'And what of Rodor?' She nodded over to where the man and the warriors who had been practising around him were watching them from the far end of the field. 'Will he also have to give up control, or is it only me?'

Vidar licked his lips, stalling for time. She was prodding him and the worst part was that she was right. He hadn't even considered wresting control from Rodor. In fact, he'd planned to welcome Rodor as a sort of second-in-command to help guide the Saxons until Vidar had gained their trust. 'You're my wife, Gwendolyn. Your place is not out here on the sparring field.'

To his surprise, she smiled sweetly. 'I see we're back to that again. Why don't you admit that this isn't about who controls the warriors? This is about you controlling me. We can leave the warriors out of it and settle it between ourselves right now. Choose your weapon.'

He smiled back, admiring her fire despite himself. 'Nay, woman, we'll settle what's between us in our bed, not in front of our warriors.'

She gritted her teeth and her cheeks turned pink. He knew she was remembering the morning and so was he. He saw her fighting him, not because she didn't want sex with him, but because she wanted to be in control of it. They were rolling in the blankets, fighting for dominance. Winning by sheer superiority of his strength, he'd come out on top and pin her down before riding her so hard that she cried out for more.

She clearly wasn't having the same fantasy. Yet. Drawing herself up to her full height, she said, 'I've already told you, that's not an option. We'll settle this with weapons.'

He stepped forward, closing the short distance between them and pulling her up against his chest. She looked ready to physically fight her way out of his arms, until he spoke. 'I'll not raise a weapon against my own wife and you'll not continue to defy me in front of the men. We'll settle this in our chamber with you beneath me before this is over.'

Her body went rigid and deathly still. She looked torn between the urge to either strike him or give him a tongue lashing he'd not soon forget, but as soon as she opened her mouth, a cry sounded from outside the open gates.

Vidar let her go and turned to find the source of the sound. There was a lookout posted at the top of the wall near the gates. He cried out again, a shrill cry that carried through the suddenly dead air.

'What's happening?' Vidar asked.

Gwendolyn was already running towards the sentry, sword in her hand, when she called back over her shoulder, 'Someone's coming.'

By the time he caught up with her, she'd already reached the bottom of the ladder that led up the wall and was talking to the man in a language he'd never heard before. He stood a bit awestruck with the ease in which she conversed with the man, who wasn't much more than a boy with barely any stubble on his jaw now that he got a better look at him. The boy stared back at him through a grime-covered face before he returned his gaze to his mistress.

'What is he saying?'

She had the nerve to wave him off as she replied to the boy in that strange tongue.

He clenched his teeth and smacked his hand against his thigh with impatience as he waited. 'Rodor!' The man had come running over with everyone else and stood at the gates. 'Do you see anyone?'

The man shook his head. 'Not yet.' Then he nodded to the conversation Gwendolyn and the boy were having. 'Sounds like it's those blasted Danes.' Realising that he was addressing one of those 'blasted Danes', he paled. 'I mean those Danes that Jarl Eirik said had been plaguing the countryside. The rebels.'

Vidar cursed. The rebels were a band of useless warriors who'd either been too indolent to earn their place as warriors, or too disrespectful to have been tolerated by their leaders. Some were even criminals who'd been banished for their crimes. It seemed the men had banded together and had nothing better to do with their time than roam the forest causing trouble. They probably had no ships to sail so were landlocked until they could earn enough money to either purchase one or have one built.

Magnus had run into them because they'd been terrorising the village home of his Saxon woman. He'd fought them back in the autumn and had won. Vidar had assumed most of them had been killed or imprisoned. Apparently, he'd been mistaken. Though he didn't consider them much of a threat, he didn't like the idea of them out roaming the territory so close to Alvey farms. Men like that wouldn't hesitate to kill an entire family for the few sheep they'd be able to scrounge.

Gwendolyn had finished talking to the boy and turned to address the men. By this time Eirik had come out and was walking up to join the group.

'Gwendolyn.' Vidar spoke harshly and gained her attention. 'What does the boy say? Is it the rebel Danes?'

To her credit, she didn't seem resentful that he'd asked, only so focused on her task that she'd forgotten he was there. The knowledge stung his pride, even while he appreciated her focus. 'Aye, they've been spotted five leagues to the south-east,' she explained. 'There are roughly two score, though a smaller band of them was seen closer. One of the farms has been sacked. Thankfully, the family was here for the wedding. The man they'd left behind to watch the sheep hid in the forest when he saw them coming, so no one was harmed.'

Another voice in the distant woods called out, interrupting her. Vidar realised that's how the boy had received his initial communication. They must have a string of lookouts in the trees and the messages passed from one to the other until it made its way to the gates.

'Get ready to go out in a quarter-hour!' she called out to her warriors. 'We'll take half, the rest stay back in case of potential attack.'

Vidar glanced at her, a bit shocked that she'd call out orders while he and the Jarl were standing right there, but her men obeyed. Apparently they knew which men would be going and which would stay back as they ran back to get their weapons and the packs they must travel with. His own men seemed to be awaiting his command, so he nodded his head. 'We'll go out. Prepare for battle.' And his men hurried to get themselves ready.

For some reason he couldn't begin to fathom, his brother stood there wearing a smile. 'She's impressive, isn't she?'

Vidar snorted as he walked towards the hall and Eirik fell into step beside him.

'Admit it, Brother. She's got them well trained.'

Vidar rolled his eyes skywards and nodded. 'Aye, fine, she has them well trained.'

'You don't seem impressed,' Eirik said.

'As if you would be impressed if Merewyn had challenged your command and tried to control your warriors?' Vidar asked.

'She did challenge my command.' Eirik shook his head, the smile momentarily dropping from his face. 'But it's not the same. Merewyn was my slave.

Had she been in control of her manor and its men, I'd have had to handle her differently.'

Vidar silently acknowledged the truth of that. 'I admit it's impressive that she's a woman and has trained the men to follow her. I give her that. But it doesn't matter. She's a wife and her place is here.' He raised his hands to indicate the hall they had just stepped inside. 'Not out there running around the countryside looking for rebels.'

A gasp drew him up short and he turned to see his wife standing there. Her sword was in its sheath strapped to her back and she held a satchel. 'You don't think I can battle them, do you?'

Vidar drew in a breath and hoped for patience. 'It's not that I think you cannot battle them. It's that you *should not* battle them.'

'But I will. I have,' she said, her legs eating up the distance between them.

Mindful of the eyes of the servants and some of the wedding guests who had waited to eat their morning meal after the warriors, he said, 'Let's discuss this in our chamber.'

'Nay.' She glanced over her shoulder at the stairway as if it were something to be fearful of and he hated that he'd taunted her about taming her in bed. Perhaps he'd been too harsh. He'd never force himself on her. 'I have fought them before and won,' she explained. 'Two winters ago they lured my brother and my betrothed into a trap and they were both killed.'

His eyes narrowed. This was the first he was hearing about a betrothed and an unreasonable pang of jealousy darted through his chest.

'I led the men out and we found their camp,' she continued. 'We killed them all and I did that. It wasn't Rodor, though he came along. It was me leading the men and calling the battle.'

A glance to his brother's face confirmed that Eirik thought he should tread carefully. His brow was furrowed and he gave a subtle nod of his head. Vidar sighed. 'Aye, I understand. You did that.' If he were in her place, he supposed that he'd be very unhappy to have someone else come into his home and usurp his authority. 'Fine. When I come back, we can talk and figure out a way to move forward. We'll figure out a way to share the responsibilities. Fair?'

She still frowned at him, her lush bottom lip sticking out a bit, and he had the strange urge to pull her into his arms and kiss her until she wasn't sad any more. She was doing something to him that he didn't understand. She was making him care about her feelings. Putting his hands on his hips to keep from kissing her, he said, 'I vow to you that we'll come up with an arrangement we're both happy with.'

He even did what he'd never done with a woman. He offered her his arm just as if she was one of his warriors.

She looked at it as if it might be a trick, but finally she relented and put her arm in his hand, grasping his arm just below the elbow. She nodded and mumbled a thank you.

Breathing a sigh of relief that they'd at least come to a hesitant peace, he said, 'So you'll stay here and make sure things are taken care of? We need some-one here in case they attack.'

She hesitated and then nodded again. 'I'll make certain everything is taken care of here.'

He smiled and almost kissed her before he thought better of it. He'd take the victory as he had it and go. No need to get her all riled up again. Some-where along the way he'd figure out how to give her just enough responsibility with the warriors that she'd leave him alone.

Gwendolyn waited until the warriors had all disappeared into the forest before going up to her chamber and packing her own satchel. She found it ridiculous that she not be allowed to go after these criminals who were trespassing on land the Alveys were in charge of protecting. She was an Alvey and she was responsible for the safety of all of her peo-ple. Had the Danes not arrived three days ago, then it would have been her duty to go out and see to the criminals. The only thing that had changed was that she was married now. In theory, that should mean that the Alvey defences were stronger. But it did not because her husband was daft and couldn't see past his own insecurity to appreciate how helpful she could be.

It was his loss, but she wouldn't stand around wringing her hands and waiting for him to realise his mistake while her people suffered. She'd heard from his orders as he left that he would be taking his Dane warriors and half of her Saxons, led by Rodor, to find the encampment of the larger group of rebels. That left the handful of rebels who'd sacked the farm still out there somewhere, potentially raiding another farm.

Filling her pack with a change of trousers and some crusts of bread and root vegetables from the hearth, she slung it over her shoulder and hurried to the armoury. On the way she called out to Wulf and four of the men who'd been left behind and told them to get ready to go with her. Wulf had been at her side the day she'd fought the men who killed Cedric and Cam. She trusted him as she trusted no other besides Rodor to fight with her.

The morning air was alive with the excitement of the event. People stood in groups chatting about what had happened and what it might mean. Everyone had been told to stay inside the gates rather than return to their homes and many of them were frightened that their homes might not be there when they were eventually allowed to return.

Annis and her husband Eadward had been talking to one of these groups of people when they heard her call out to her men. Gwendolyn grimaced at their attention and then silently cursed as they broke away from the group and hurried over to her. She didn't wait for them, though, and hurried inside the armoury to stock her quiver with arrows and retrieve her crossbow.

'Gwendolyn, what in God's name are you doing?' Annis asked when she burst through the open door. Eadward followed on her heels, the deep frown on his face conveying his displeasure.

'Blasphemy, Annis? I'm disappointed in you,' Gwendolyn teased her sister as she lifted her crossbow down from its shelf.

'Do not quibble with me.' The raised tone of her voice made Gwendolyn realise just how upset her sister was.

Sighing, Gwendolyn turned her full attention on her sister and Eadward. The crossbow hung loosely at her side as she said, 'I'm going to find the criminals burning our farms.'

'But your husband just took men to do exactly that.'

'Aye, he did. Only he's taken men to find the large encampment. I'm going to find the small group terrorising our farms. Vidar can have the larger battle. I'll be quite content rooting out the others,' Gwendolyn explained.

'Your husband told you to stay home,' Eadward said, surprising her by stepping forward. His voice was deep, but quiet and reserved. 'You should do as he's told you.' When Annis nodded her head in agreement, Gwendolyn rolled her eyes.

'I'll not stay here when I could better serve my people by going out with my men.'

'Did you not promise to obey your husband only yesterday?' he asked.

'Aye, but I promised to defend my people long before I made that vow.' She was getting tired of people behaving as if she'd given up her right to defend Alvey just because of her marriage. 'The whole point of this marriage was to make Alvey stronger.'

Eadward's gaze wavered and she knew that her argument made sense to him. 'It doesn't seem right,' he said, though his voice had lost some of its firmness.

Stepping forward, she put her hand on his arm and gave it a squeeze. 'I'm only trying to do what's right for our people. If I can find the small group terrorising the farms, then I can potentially stop another farm from being destroyed. Please stay here until I return. Help to defend the gates if it comes to it.' She turned to Annis. 'Please watch the hall. Do what you're best at and keep everyone calm and occupied in one activity or another so they won't worry. You're better at that than I. If I stay, I'll only make everyone anxious with my pacing. I need to do something. I need to do this.' She raised her crossbow up to show them.

Much to her relief Annis nodded and Eadward stepped back out of the way. Giving them both a hug, she ran out the door and went to collect her horse and her men. The thrill of the hunt already zinging through her veins, she felt useful again.

Chapter Nine

Vidar paced the walkway that had been built near the top of the wall, waiting for some sign that his wife would make it home that day. He'd left on the morning two days ago with implicit orders for her to keep herself at home, but when he'd returned just hours ago, he'd found out that she'd defied him almost immediately after he'd left. The anger he'd felt at being so blatantly defied was indescribable. He'd never felt such a rage. No one under his command had ever outright defied a direct order. It wasn't done, because it could be dangerous. He'd tried to reason with her before leaving. Had even promised her that they would come to an equitable agreement, but she'd thrown that in his face. It was time the woman learned her place.

The sun was setting in the west, casting long shadows across the open terrain that the wall looked out on. The Saxons left behind had told him that she'd ridden out to the east with her men. She hadn't followed Vidar; it seemed she'd been in pursuit of that small band of men who'd been burning farms. Despite himself, now that he'd had time to consider that detail, he had to admit that he was worried for her as much as he was angry. She infuriated him as no woman ever had, but he didn't wish her harmed.

On the evening of their first day out hunting the rebel Danes, a rainstorm had come. It had been so swiftly upon them and had come down so hard, they'd been forced to shelter in the trees. Though the trees hadn't done much to keep them dry and warm once night had fallen. They'd pressed on with the morning light, but by the time they'd reached the camp, it had been cleared and any trail had been lost with the continuing rain. Nevertheless, Vidar and the men had searched for signs, but it had become apparent that the rebels had headed off in smaller groups to cover their tracks and the rain had aided them.

Fearful that the continuing rain would cause the streams and rivers to swell so much that they'd be rendered too dangerous to traverse, they'd returned home so that Eirik could take his men and leave on their ships. Now Vidar stood upon the wall, afraid that his bride had been swept away in one of those streams, or perhaps even killed by the rebels. Or, even worse, taken captive by the rebels who could even now be using her harshly for their own pleasure.

He wiped a hand over his brow to smite out the thought. The air was still heavy with the damp left over from the rain and the smell of wet earth. The wind had turned cold now that the clouds had passed. He'd debated having men ride out to look for her at least a dozen times, but her tracks would be long gone. Yet he felt helpless waiting here for some sign of her and he didn't like the feeling. Behind that sentiment was the nagging sense that he'd failed to keep her safe. She'd been his wife for less than a sennight and he'd already failed her.

He stared out at the emptiness of the forest across the field. By the gods, if she came through the gates right now he'd relish her punishment. He'd flog her in the sparring field for all to see. But as soon as he thought it, he realised that was simply the anger talking. He'd meant it when he'd said that their disputes should be handled in their chamber away from the warriors.

He wouldn't flog her. He'd take her to their chamber and spank her until her buttocks turned red, so that she'd remember the consequences of defiance. The fact that he went rigid in his trousers simply thinking about the punishment didn't figure into it. It was about keeping her in line for her own safety, not his own pleasure. Even though the thought of exerting his control over her in such a way left his blood simmering in his veins. In his mind, she enjoyed receiving the punishment as much as he'd enjoyed giving it to her. Her cries of outrage turned to moans of pleasure as she squirmed in his lap.

The pink imprint of his hand on her pale buttocks branded her as his.

'My lord!'

The call dragged Vidar from his thoughts and made him realise he'd closed his eyes to better live out the fantasy in his mind. The boy who'd been lookout the day they'd learned about the rebel Danes approached him.

'Look there. We've received word that Lady Gwendolyn comes.' The boy pointed to a break in the trees, but nothing was there. A messenger must have called out to alert them that she was coming, but Vidar had been too deep in his own thoughts to notice.

Shaking his head and cursing under his breath, he said, 'Has she been spotted with her men?'

'Aye, she appears unharmed.'

'Send her to me in the hall when she comes. She's not to go to the armoury or the stable yard.' He tried to ignore the relief moving through him, but it was nearly palpable. She was well and for the moment that's all that mattered.

Gwendolyn rode through the gates with her head held high and her quiver of arrows nearly empty. She and her men had picked up the rebels' tracks and found them despite the heavy downpour. The rain had even helped her to get the upper hand. She and the men had been able to hide in the trees while the rain hid their sounds from the criminals. It had been difficult and excruciatingly slow climbing up the slick, wet bark of the trees, but they'd managed it. Then they'd had to wait for the men to come out of the hastily built cover of limbs they'd made to shelter from the rain. Finally, one by one they had made an appearance to relieve themselves in the woods.

Arrows from her crossbow had taken out three of them before the trio left inside the shelter had figured out what was happening. The rebels didn't have arrows to fight back, so they'd simply made a run for it to get to their horses. But Gwendolyn had anticipated the move and had men who'd circled around the makeshift camp to wait for them at their horses. In the end, her group was able to take out all six of the rebels and obtain their horses and supplies.

Vidar had only brought horses for himself and his best men, leaving the rest of his small army to travel on foot or by boat. Therefore, Alvey needed all the horses it could get.

She and her men had even managed to collect the stolen sheep the rebels had taken and had brought them back to be returned to the farmer. The sheep had slowed their progress returning to Alvey, so Gwendolyn had spent the entire trip hoping that Vidar had not already returned home.

One look at the reactions of the men around the yard when she rode in told her that he had beaten her back. She recognised a few of the Danes as those who'd ridden with him. Even Rodor was at the fire near the outdoor kitchen. He was busy charming the widow in charge of the meals for the hall, but he frowned the moment he saw Gwendolyn ride in. The other Danes glared at her with a contempt that shocked her. From the scowls on their faces, she'd almost think they were angry with her. What reason did they have to be angry?

Well, this was certain to be an interesting night. One of the boys ran out to help her with her horse, but she waved him off. 'Get some boys and keep an eye on the sheep. I'll need to alert their master so that he can see to them properly for the evening.'

'That won't be necessary,' said Rodor, drawing her gaze to him as he made his way towards her. His next words were directed to the boy. 'Go tell Aethelbert that the mistress has found his sheep.'

The boy nodded and ran off. Gwendolyn sighed and dismounted there rather than ride the horse to the stable as it appeared Rodor had words for her. He walked up and took the reins from her, his frown even more disapproving than Eadward's had been before she left to chase the rebels.

'Say what you have to say and be done with it,' she urged.

'You know what I have to say. You should not have defied your husband.' Rodor kept his voice low, but everyone was watching them with interest.

'Aye, that's what I thought you would say. You'll be happy to know that we found the rebels who burned Aethelbert's farm. They won't be bothering us any more.'

'I had no doubt you would.' He inclined his head with the respect she was accustomed to from him, leaving her wondering exactly what he was so upset about.

'Then why do you look as if I'm about to hang for my crimes?'

He glanced around to the Danes. 'Because you are to be punished for disobeying your lord husband.'

She nearly laughed aloud at that, but stopped herself when she realised that he wasn't teasing her. The Danes had yet to look away from her and some of them looked absolutely menacing with their scowls. 'Perhaps I did disobey him, but it was for the greater need of our people.'

He nodded, but she had the sneaking suspicion that he didn't believe it changed anything. 'Aye, I understand. But the greater need of your people, right now, is to see that their master and their mistress are united. The Saxons don't appreciate what your father did any more than you do. You might bear the greater burden having to share your bed with a Northman, but our men are asked to share their hall with these strangers we once called enemies. They're asked to share their duties, their meals, their entertainment, and soon…their women.'

'Their women? Rodor, I assure you that I would never allow…'

He shook his head. 'Nay, I mean that the Danes didn't bring women with them. It appears that most of them are unwed. What do you think will happen? They'll start to compete for the attention of our Saxon women. I'm not sure you've noticed, but we haven't enough to go around.'

Gwendolyn grimaced and glanced around. Except for the female servants working at the kitchen, she only saw men. Rodor was probably right. There was one woman for at least every two men, not counting the surrounding farms. She assumed the Danes would eventually want to wed. But she also noticed something else, something that disturbed her even more than that. The Danes all stared at her with anger, but the Saxon men only stared at her with concern. Yet, when they glanced at the Danes, anger flashed in their eyes and she could see that a storm was brewing. If she didn't tread carefully, it could come down to her Saxons against Vidar's Danes and she feared for the damage to her people if that battle ever took place.

All at once the weight of the responsibility she had thought she'd learned to bear long ago suddenly felt ten times heavier. She'd learned to trust her instincts and to carefully consider her situation. Yet in this situation, her instincts were not true. She wanted to fight against Vidar's imposed dominance, but she couldn't. At least not in the way that she had been fighting.

'I didn't expect Vidar or his men to be happy about my disobedience, but the fact that I brought back six horses and recovered the stolen sheep ought to count for something.'

Rodor shrugged. 'Perhaps it will, but you'll have to speak with your husband about that. He's waiting for you in the hall and I suggest you not keep him any longer.'

Gwendolyn took in a deep breath and left Rodor to care for her horse as she made her way to the hall. She could feel every eye in the yard on her, so she kept her back straight and her step surefooted. In her heart, she knew that she was in the right here and that she had done exactly what she had needed to do to ensure the safety of her people. Because of her actions, those rebels weren't out there any more raiding farms. The fact that she was right did nothing to stop her heart from pounding so hard that the blood roared in her ears.

The door to the hall was open, so she stepped inside, hoping against hope that she'd be able to cross the large room and make it to the stairs in the back without being seen. It was a foolish hope, but the knowledge didn't stop her from holding her breath as she stepped inside as if that might make her less noticeable. She'd much prefer their confrontation to happen in private.

Apparently every person in the room had been eagerly anticipating her arrival, because they all stopped to stare at her. She realised then how utterly foolish her little hope had been. Of course the lookout had told everyone she had returned. Even if he hadn't, one of the angry Danes from outside had surely come in to alert his master.

As if it were lightning drawn to steel, her gaze found Vidar's across the distance of the room. He was sitting at the head of the table on the bench made for the both of them. Her spot was empty, but his friend—Rolfe, she thought his name was—sat to his right. In fact, the whole table was nothing but Danes and something about that made her heart stop in her chest and anger flush her cheeks. He could not come into her home and completely take it over. She had come to terms with having to share it with him and his men, but it would not be his alone. Her men had earned their place at her table.

'Good evening, Wife. It's good to have you home,' Vidar called out, his voice cutting through the sudden silence. When she didn't make a move, Vidar stood. 'Come. Have a drink.'

He raised the goblet that they had used to drink their honeyed mead from on the night of their wedding. She'd forgotten it, but remembered he'd said that tradition demanded that they drink from it every night for the month. In an effort to keep the peace, she walked over to the table and reached for the goblet. He only smiled and shook his head, preferring to hold it up to her lips himself. She dutifully took a sip and he waited until she was finished before taking a drink himself, making sure to place his lips where hers had been.

'We've missed the last few nights. Some would

call that a foreboding of ill things to come or bad luck. But I prefer to think of this as a new beginning.' He raised the goblet up and looked out across the men at the table. 'From this night forward, we'll agree to start again. We'll put aside our differences and begin anew as husband and wife, master and mistress, lord and lady.' When he ended, his gaze had come back to settle on her. She wasn't certain if his brief speech had been meant for his men's favour or if he meant it.

The weight of his gaze was nearly palpable. Gwendolyn sensed a trap of some kind. Vidar was supposed to be angry. Rodor had indicated as much and the Danes outside had certainly been upset. He didn't appear overly put out, though. Unless he was one of those men who stifled his anger until it exploded in a storm of thunder and rained down on everyone around him. She hadn't thought that was the case. Not with the way he'd been so direct with her up until now.

'Aye,' she replied, glancing out over the Danes who seemed to be awaiting her reaction. 'I agree that we should start anew. I'd like for our joining to be a true joining of our people.'

'Wonderful,' Vidar said, setting his goblet down without retaking his seat. 'Are you hungry, my wife? Would you like to sit with us and eat?'

She shook her head. 'I'm more tired than hungry, my lord.' She'd thought that she'd have to force the title out, but it actually came very easily. Quite pleased with herself, she smiled. 'I'd rather retire for the evening.'

'Then we should get to your punishment, so that you can retire. I'm sure you're exhausted from your travels.'

Those words settled between them with a dull thud. 'My punishment?' Her heart picked up speed.

'Aye. You defied my direct command. The warriors under my command who defy my orders are punished. So you, too, shall be punished.'

She nearly had to drag her chin off the floor to answer him. 'As you've been so eager to point out, I am not a warrior, I am your wife.'

He grinned, one corner of his mouth tipping up in a smirk that left her palm tingling to slap it away. 'Then as my wife you should be punished for defying me.'

She gasped aloud, but tried to stifle her voice so that it wouldn't carry. 'How dare you give me false words of a fresh start and then bring punishment into this?'

'Oh, I'll dare much more than that, my lady. We've agreed to a fresh start, but you must be punished for your crimes before we can begin. Tomorrow, I swear to you it will be as if it never happened, but I cannot allow disrespect to go unpunished.'

'Nay.' She shook her head and started backing up. 'I won't allow it.'

He didn't seem phased by her objection. He nodded and took a step towards her. 'Then I'm afraid

I have no choice.' Before she realised what he intended, he picked her up and slung her over his shoulder like a sack of wheat and strode towards the stairs. To her everlasting mortification, the Danes in the hall let out a cheer that nearly shook the rafters.

Gwendolyn had no idea what his idea of punishment might be, so she fought him the entire way, not that it did much good. He seemed strong enough to deal with her flailing and traverse the steep stairway at the same time. Pushing the heavy wooden door of their chamber open, he kicked it closed behind him and walked towards the bed, depositing her on top as if she didn't weigh a thing. Her braid had come undone during the struggle, so she pushed it out of her face as she sat up, prepared to fight him off of her.

He stood at the foot of the bed, calmly taking off his tunic and tossing it aside, but he made no move to discard the rest of his clothes. 'Take off your trousers,' he said.

'Are you mad? I will do no such thing. Need I remind you that you said you would never force yourself on me?'

'I have no plans to force myself on you. Take off your trousers. Now.' His face was hard and impassive, and his hands had come to rest on his hips.

Shaking her head, she shuffled backwards until her back came up against the headboard. 'I'll have no part of this punishment. How dare you punish me anyway? Aye, I defied you, but I killed the small group of rebels raiding our farms. I brought back six horses for our warriors along with the farmer's sheep. If I were a man, you would be praising my task.'

He smiled, but it held no humour. 'If you were a man, I would not call you wife, so, aye, perhaps I would praise you. But that's not who you are. You *are* my wife and you defied me. More than that, you put your life in danger and I had no idea if you were injured or killed. For all I knew, you'd been taken captive by those cowards.'

Was it possible he'd worried about her? The thought had barely crossed her mind before he fell to his knees on to the end of the bed and started coming towards her. At that point, she had more pressing concerns. 'What are you doing? What is this punishment?' Her voice rose on the end, because if she was being honest with herself she was as alarmed as she was angry.

'You defied me like a child, so I will punish you as I would a child. You lied to me and put your safety at risk. Had that not been the case, then I could overlook it. But what you did was extreme, Gwendolyn. You could be dead and I would be responsible in the eyes of all of Alvey.'

He looked so earnest that she entertained the notion that maybe she could make him understand. 'That's ridiculous. No one would fault you. I left on my own. I chose to go. You share no responsibility for that.'

'But I do. I swore to protect you at the ceremony,

even if my own life called for it. I swore to these people to hold your life above my own. And I meant it.' His eyes were such a vivid blue as they peered into hers that for a moment she actually believed he might care for her. 'I have to do whatever I can to ensure your safety, even if that means disciplining you when you do things to put yourself at risk. I'm sorry, but I have to punish you.' He reached forward and grabbed her arms, pulling her across the bed as easily as if she were a child's wooden doll.

She tried to jerk away, but there was no question he was stronger than she was. His grip didn't budge and she felt the first real stirrings of fear that this might actually happen. Up until now, she hadn't considered his discipline as a real possibility. 'What do you mean, punish me like a child?'

'You'll soon find out.' He spoke through a clenched jaw and her mind went through all the ways she'd been reprimanded as a child. None of them had ever been physical. Being sent to bed without her supper had been the most extreme. Or there was that time she'd taken her brother's dagger without asking and bent the blade on a rock when she'd been practising throwing at targets in the dirt. He'd threatened to turn her over his knee, but her father had intervened before he'd done it.

Her eyes widened as she realised that's exactly what this barbarian meant to do to her. 'I am not a child.'

'Don't act like a child and you won't be punished

like one.' Apparently tired of her struggling away from him, he gave a yank and pulled her off balance so that she fell against his chest. They paused for a moment, knee to knee, chest to breasts. He held her wrists locked at the small of her back with both of his. She tugged hard enough to wrench her wrists, but she couldn't loosen his hold. An unwelcomed thrill of excitement shot through her and it was as unexpected as it was jarring. His shrewd blue eyes locked with hers and she realised that he wasn't even panting yet. He'd nearly subdued her with so little effort she would have been more afraid if she wasn't so impressed by his sheer power. She could barely stomach the thought, but there was something appealing about his superior strength.

'Taking my warriors to fight bad men intent on destroying property and potentially taking lives is not the act of a child.'

'You are correct.' His voice had lowered. He stared down into her eyes and, even though she was so angry at him, she was struck by the attractiveness of his features. His clear blue eyes, square jaw and straight nose. It really was too bad that he had to be so unreasonable. She watched his perfect lips as he said, 'It was an impressive accomplishment.'

It was probably as close to a compliment as she would get from him. Her mouth fell open and his gaze dipped down to her lips. An awareness moved between them with that look. It said that he found her as attractive as she found him. It said that if circumstances were different, they might enjoy each other very much.

This was madness. He was her enemy. Blinking to clear her thoughts, she said, 'Do you really think so?' She hated herself for needing to hear his praise. It shouldn't matter what this Dane thought of her, but something within her longed to hear his approval of her.

His gaze jumped back up and when it connected to hers the intensity of it called to that longing deep within her. His eyes weren't raging any more. They had suddenly become bottomless and solemn, and that was immensely appealing to her. A mere barbarian couldn't look at her that way. 'I do. You took out a group of enemies who meant to harm us. And you did it without loss of life while enriching us in the process. It's admirable…for a warrior.'

She swallowed, her stomach churning in dread, because she already knew what he would say next. 'But not admirable for a wife?'

Shaking his head, he said, 'But not a wife. Especially one who disobeyed her husband.' She only realised that his grip had become slack when he tightened it again. 'For that, I'm going to spank you.'

Chapter Ten

Gwendolyn struggled away from him, intent on getting out of his grasp before he could spank her. She attempted to bring her knee up, but he was too close and it was as if his thighs were made of iron. 'You will not do this!' she screamed.

He sighed—*sighed!*—as if she were a minor annoyance and he'd much rather get on with his evening than deal with her. 'If you'd co-operate, this would move along much faster and we could be done with it.' His breath whooshed out on the last breath because she managed to get her shoulder into his stomach.

She didn't have time to indulge her minor victory, however, as she had to turn to try to pull out of his grasp. She managed to get one arm free from his grip, but he recovered quickly and tightened his hold on her other wrist. Jerking away, she got him off balance and he fell forward, but his larger frame fell on to her, effectively stopping her bid to escape from the bed.

He'd released her, but it hardly mattered as she was face down in the blanket and his heavy torso was pinning her beneath him. Dear Lord, the man must weigh the same as a horse. She squirmed to get out from under him and her bottom came into contact with his groin. She pressed back as it was the only leverage she had and realised it wasn't simply his groin she wiggled against, but his rather large male appendage. The shock of it left her as stiff as his erection.

Immediately, she dropped her hips to break the contact, but the pulse between her thighs fluttered to life and tendrils of eager anticipation wound their way through her entire body. Her eyes fell closed as she fought the instinct to push back against him again, to savour the strangely satisfying feel of his hard length pressed against the softness of her bottom. The pulse beat an insistent rhythm in that soft place made for him.

Do not feel anything for him but disgust. Do not physically yearn for him.

He panted above her—*panted* when just moments ago he hadn't. She was almost certain it was because of his condition rather than fatigue from their brief skirmish. The bulk of his weight still resting on her back, his hips came down on to her bottom to hold her still. He shifted to get a better position with his knee, but the result was that it pressed his erection very firmly against a plump cheek. His breath blew past her ear in what she was certain was an unintentional caress, but it made a shiver of pleasure run down her spine. She nearly groaned at the resulting ache deep in her centre. Even her breasts were full and achy, and her nipples were hard as they pressed against the bed.

'Do you submit?' His voice was soft, but held a husky note that raked across her senses. It prickled her skin and caused a flutter of response in her belly.

'Never.' The word was muffled against the blanket as she squeezed her eyes shut tighter and willed away the terrible effect he was having on her body. She was coming to recognise his scent, a mixture of leather and pine along with something that was distinctly him. And it floated around her now, seeping into her pores and feeding her desire.

She didn't want this. She didn't want him. It was no use though. No matter how she tried to fight it, she *enjoyed* having him above her. She *enjoyed* his body on hers. She even *enjoyed* the fact that he was physically stronger than her. This man wanted to keep her in her place as a mere wife and still she was attracted to him. It felt so wrong, but that wickedness only fed the attraction.

All of those thoughts flew out of her head when he grabbed for the waist of her trousers. Her eyes flew open and she pressed herself up with her hands. His chest still held her down, so she didn't get far. 'What are you doing?'

'I can't properly spank you with fabric between us.' That same husk was present in his voice and it sent a shard of pleasure straight to her core. God help her. He tugged, but she was lying on the fastenings so they wouldn't budge. She knew now, though, that he'd be able to toss her over on to her back with no problem and he'd take the trousers off her if he wanted to. If he did it that way, then he'd no doubt see her *there* between her legs. He'd see the wetness there and know his effect on her. She'd die from the humiliation if she had to endure him seeing her down there, knowing she was aroused, and a spanking.

He moved up on to his knees and grabbed her hips to do just that, she was certain. Panic sent her heart racing in her chest, so she acted first. 'Wait! I'll submit.' He paused, but his hands didn't leave her hips. 'Just let me do it,' she urged.

He still didn't budge and she thought perhaps his goal was to humiliate her further, but he finally moved off her. She flipped over and narrowed her gaze at him. He kept a cool, level eye on her as he moved to sit on the side of the bed. Then he held his hands up as if to say he was waiting for her.

Sitting up in bed, she slowly moved back away from him towards the headboard and his gaze narrowed. She knew that she'd have to play him carefully or he'd do what he wanted whether she liked it or not. 'I promise to co-operate if you allow me to keep my trousers.'

'Nay.' He shook his head and his jaw tightened. The fire was back in his eyes and she suspected that he enjoyed this little game of theirs. Well, his erection had told her that earlier, hadn't it?

Clenching her teeth, she said, 'Fine, but I won't take them off. I'll simply pull them down…a little.'

He gave a slight inclination of his head and she knew it was the only concession she was likely to get. Slowly she got to her feet and walked the few steps to reach him. If he'd been smug or had even a glimmer of victory in his eye, she might have run for the door and faced the inevitable consequences. But he merely sat there calmly…and waited, his broad chest rising and falling with his breath as he stared at her. When she paused next to him, he didn't make a move to force her down. He still waited.

She brought her hands to the waistband of her trousers, but paused. 'Do you… Can you make it quick? Please?'

His gaze was solemn and almost kind when he said, 'It's not my intention to hurt you unduly.'

'Then why must we—?'

'Enough.' His harsh order cut through her words. 'Let us get this over with.'

Biting her lip to stop her words, lest she disgrace herself by begging or saying angry words that would make him harsher, she hastily unfastened her trousers and held both sides with her hands. He patted his thigh and she placed herself over them, awkwardly keeping a grip on her trousers. His legs were like tree trunks beneath her, hard and unyielding. Apparently not enough of her rear was exposed, because he yanked the trousers down until she could feel the waistband on the backs of her thighs exposing her to God and himself. She closed her eyes against the embarrassment. No one had seen her nude bottom since she'd been a child.

She gritted her teeth against what she knew was coming and her whole body clenched. But the first thing she felt wasn't a hard thwack. It was his warm palm coming to rest on one cheek. She flinched in shock and her eyes flew open at the unexpectedly gentle contact. He smoothed his hand over first one side and then the other, stoking this fire of arousal that had momentarily been dampened by her humiliation. Her nipples tightened and her skin tingled where he touched. The muscles low in her belly clenched.

She closed her eyes and allowed herself to be lulled by his hand. She wanted to know what he was thinking as he looked at her. As his palm moved, his fingertips traced little waves that soothed her. She realised that he was keeping her waiting, because it was his way of taking all control from her. He wouldn't start based on her prompting. Everything was quite literally in his hands now. There was nothing to do now but wait and she found herself relaxing under his touch.

Somewhere so deep inside her she'd never even known it was there, a part of her liked how he took control. There was something about his domination that was freeing. She didn't have to be in charge of everything. He was strong enough to take some of the responsibility that had weighed on her for the past two years. She'd liked bearing the needs of her people, but only as the weight of the burden was lifted a little did she understand how heavy it had been.

Perhaps this wasn't a spanking after all. Perhaps this was simply to teach her a lesson about trusting him. Perhaps he meant to caress— *Thwack!* The slap was so unexpected that she cried out, more from the shock than the pain. Though heat rose across her skin where she was certain an imprint of his hand lingered, it hadn't hurt...exactly.

'Do you promise not to lie to me again?' His hand rested on her bottom as he spoke and it was distracting because his thumb moved in a lazy back-and-forth stroke that seemed to be soothing the redness he'd almost surely left behind. As it soothed, it also caused excitement to stir in her blood.

She was so confused. Was this a punishment or a seduction? 'What do you mean? I didn't lie—'

A second thwack cut off her words. This time on her other cheek and her skin tingled with the heat of pain. 'Do you promise?'

'I didn't—' There was no caress that time as he smacked her again. She tried to reach back to cover herself, but he put his left arm over her back, and his hand pressed her arm to her body, keeping her still. Something inside her thrilled at the domination.

'You did lie to me. You told me you'd stay home and you left,' he explained. His hand rested on her bottom, his palm rubbing in a circle, soothing the minor burning. She squirmed, but it was because the stinging pain was getting all twisted with the pleasure. Somehow it was all comingling and winding the pleasure tighter inside her. She rubbed her thighs together to quell the ache between them.

This was Vidar, a Dane, a man she should not want! She tried to fight it, but the pleasure was there whether she wanted it or not. Perhaps if he smacked her again the pain would outweigh the pleasure once and for all, and settle the war raging in her body. 'Nay, I did not lie.' He obliged her. This thwack was the loudest yet and it made her cry out from the sting, but it had only worked to sharpen that edge of pleasure and twist it higher.

She squirmed when he rested his palm on her bottom, trying to get closer and away from him at the same time. Her movement caused the fingertips of his last two fingers to drop into the crevice created where her bottom met her thigh. It was so close to the source of that wetness between her thighs that she was afraid he might feel it.

And what if he'd been telling the truth when he'd said that he could smell her arousal? Even thinking that he might know that this punishment was making her want him somehow made that place between her thighs begin to throb harder with a desperate need she'd never felt before. She wanted him to touch her there.

'Do not lie to me again.' He gave her a moment to speak, but must have taken her silence for defiance, because he raised his hand and smacked her again. This time it was low, near where he'd touched. She cried out as the vibrations from it moved through her aching sex. She squirmed with genuine desperation now. God help her, but she yearned for Vidar to stroke her.

Nay, she wanted that male part of him to push inside her and fill the ache. He was as rigid as he'd been earlier. She could feel him against her hip.

He paused and she braced herself for another thwack, silently begging him to do it again. But he didn't and she bit her lip to keep herself from groaning when his palm ran over her bottom and down to the backs of her thighs. His fingertip dipped down between her thighs, so close to the source of her frustration, but still not touching it. She whimpered when he pulled his hand away.

He spoke, but it was in his own language and it came out on a harsh breath. Something about the tone of his voice mixed with the foreign harshness of his words nearly sent her over the edge and made her plead with him to take her. Instead, she kept her eyes closed tight, silently begging him to touch her while at the same time hoping he wouldn't. If he did, she didn't know if she'd be able to stop herself from responding, but she had in no way come to terms with wanting him. He was her enemy, but that somehow only sweetened the allure, just like pain had become pleasure. Everything was all mixed up.

But he did touch her. She groaned aloud when his fingertips ran down the seam of the lips guarding her sex.

'You're wet for me,' he whispered, his voice filled with a strange awe that she wasn't certain how to explain.

He was right. It was all for him. How was it possible she wanted him, but hated him at the same time? What was happening to her? She shifted, unsure what she meant to do, but his other hand moved to the back of her head, his fingers tightening in her hair as he held her still. Without even thinking, she obeyed his silent command and the air left her lungs as she relaxed. He was in control, she could simply close her eyes and feel.

Two of his fingertips pushed between her lips, finding evidence of his effect on her as they slicked over her flesh. He pushed downward and she nearly jumped when he touched a part of her that was so swollen and aching, stars exploded behind her eyelids when he touched her there and her whole body pounded. 'Vidar,' she cried out softly.

'Gwendolyn.' His own voice was strained with what sounded like need as he made circles around that sensitive place.

Despite herself, she moved her hips in rhythm

to him and pressed against his erection at the same time. He muttered something beneath his breath and after a moment dragged her up from his lap. As easily as if she weighed nothing he tossed her on to the bed and came down on top of her. She didn't even think as she clutched his shoulders and welcomed the weight of his body on hers. He grabbed at her trousers, pushing them down past her knees as he came to rest between her thighs. Though his clothing was still between them, his hardness was pressed against her intimately.

Aye! She needed his hardness there. She moaned at the contact and he covered her open mouth with his. His tongue plundered her mouth, stroking against hers in a way she'd never imagined was possible. But it was exciting and answered to that inexplicable need that called for his complete possession of her. She found that she loved drinking the sweet taste of mead from his tongue.

He whispered her name again as he pulled back only enough to take in a breath and his hand found its way beneath her tunic. She knew he was intent on reaching her breasts and her nipples ached for his touch. It was as if her entire body was coming to life for him. For Vidar. And it was begging him to touch her everywhere.

Nothing like this had ever happened to her before. Not with Cam. That one time had been quick and she'd been almost fully clothed. This terrible and glorious need hadn't overtaken her.

And this wasn't Cam. This was Vidar. A Dane. A man who had tried to punish her for protecting her own people. A man who only wanted to control her.

What was wrong with her? How could she betray herself so easily? His rough palm moved up her ribcage, but she grabbed his wrist before he could touch her breast. 'Nay.'

'What?' He pushed up with his other hand to look down at her. His golden hair fell down over his strong shoulders and he looked so appealing that she very nearly pushed her principles aside. But who would she be if she gave in to him? She was too afraid to find out.

'Please stop. I don't want this.' Before he could say or do anything to sway her, she pushed hard on his shoulders and he toppled right off the bed, landing with a loud thud on the floor.

He came to his feet with a roar, as she grabbed the blanket to pull it over her. 'By the hounds of hades, what are you doing, woman?'

'I can't do this with you,' she said, steeling herself for the fight that was certain to come.

His gaze raked her from head to foot, but when he met her gaze again his eyes had softened. He wasn't angry, but he did appear confused and, if she wasn't mistaken, a little hurt. He didn't say anything. He simply nodded and ran a hand over his tousled hair. Then he retrieved his tunic from where he'd tossed it earlier before leaving the room.

She let out a breath in relief as she sank back into

144 The Viking Warrior's Bride

the pillows, her body still throbbing with need. She couldn't believe how close she'd come to betraying herself. She didn't know why, but somehow giving in to him had come to mean that he'd won this battle between them. And she couldn't allow that to happen.

Chapter Eleven

Vidar knew that he'd been too harsh with her, but he hadn't meant for her to take his action as a cruelty. Taking her over his knee had been a simple punishment. He couldn't count the times Eirik had turned him over his knee as a child. Their father's preferred method of punishment had been an open palm to the side of the head and Vidar had always hated those. They'd left him feeling dizzy and angry and rejected in a way he hadn't understood at the time. Now that he was older, he realised that the face and head were too personal. A blow to someone's face meant that you were out to do them harm and you disliked them immensely.

The arse was impersonal. A good spanking was nothing more than a lesson in obedience and respect. He didn't want to harm her and he certainly didn't dislike her. He simply wanted her to understand the severity of her mistake in lying to him and putting herself in danger.

However, when he'd gone back to their chamber last night, he'd found her asleep. She'd been curled up on her side, facing away from him, and she'd sniffled every so often, making him think that she'd cried herself to sleep. He hadn't struck her *that* hard. And she hadn't come down for the morning meal yet, so he was starting to think that perhaps he'd made things worse between them.

Or perhaps it hadn't been the spanking that had set her off. Perhaps it had been what came after—or during. Propping his elbows on the table, he dropped his chin into his hands and watched the people bustling around the room as he tried to make sense of it. Who was he trying to fool? It had never been a proper spanking from the beginning. He'd been as hard as a bloody rock since he'd tossed her on to the bed. The wrestling before the spanking had only made it worse.

Rolfe pushed back from the table, interrupting Vidar's thoughts. A wide grin was on his friend's arrogant face. 'Did the punishment not go well?'

Vidar cursed under his breath and shot a glance down the table to make sure no one was near. Most of the men had already started filing out of the hall for the sparring field. 'It went fine. Why do you ask?'

Rolfe laughed. 'The last time I saw you look so sullen was when we lost that ship on the crossing.' He gave an exaggerated shrug. 'Our ships are safe and so are the warriors. My bet is on your wife.'

'Get outside to your duties,' Vidar said between clenched teeth, unwilling to discuss his problems with his wife.

Rolfe shook his head. 'I'd rather stay here and watch the entertainment.' He nodded towards the stairs in the back of the hall and Vidar's heart faltered in his chest.

He hadn't yet figured out how to deal with her. Straightening his spine, he said, 'Go, or by the gods—' Vidar didn't even have to finish the threat, because Rolfe threw back his head and laughed as he walked towards the door.

Vidar knew a moment of uncertainty just before she reached his side. The last thing he wanted was to deal with a hysterical wife. However, he managed to put on a neutral expression as he stood. She gave him a brief nod as she stepped around him to take her place on the bench. She didn't appear angry or sad or anything. That set him on edge more than her hysterics would have.

She wore a tunic and trousers, making him think she intended to spar with her warriors this morning. His gaze caught on her arse as she slipped in front of him and he was reminded of when he'd had her across his lap. She had the most perfect arse he'd ever seen in his life. As soon as she'd draped herself over his thighs, he'd sat for a moment mesmerised at the beauty of her nude body and a little stunned to find that her bottom had been as plump as he'd imagined when he'd seen her drop out of that tree.

Her cheeks had been round and firm. He'd wanted to knead them and it had taken all of his self-control to only caress her flesh and not squeeze. He'd been so drunk on lust that he'd nearly forgotten his purpose.

But his inebriation had only worsened when he'd spanked her, because he'd underestimated how satisfying it would be to see the imprint of his hand on her pale skin, branding her as his. It was made better by the fact that she'd cried out in pleasure, not pain. She'd *liked* it and he didn't quite know what to do with that information. He'd hoped that it would lead to a night of consummating their marriage, though it hadn't.

At least he was now assured of her desire for him. He'd use that information to figure out how to get her to bed him. He could punish her and he could take privileges away from her, but nothing would put her under his control as firmly as having her submit to him. Their bed was the place to start.

'Good morning, Wife.' A swell of pride moved through him when she looked at him and blushed.

'Good morning, Vidar,' she said as she settled herself on the bench. She tried to keep her expression impassive, but she couldn't hide the pink that stole across her features.

One of the servants approached—he still hadn't learned their names, perhaps something he needed to rectify—and offered her a bowl of pottage and some meat from the night before. She accepted graciously and stared down at the food before her.

He sat down beside her and he found himself weighing the situation as he would a negotiation with a foe. It was good that she wasn't upset and had apparently reconciled herself to what had happened. But he couldn't shake the feeling that she was up to something. She was too measured and focused. What did she want and what was she willing to accept in its stead? She wanted to be in control, but that wasn't something he could give up. He had no idea how much less she was willing to accept.

Vidar gave a quick shake of his head as he determined one very important fact: he could handle an enemy better than a wife. It was best to retreat until he could figure out a way to proceed. He'd prepared himself for hysterics, not this rational creature. He started to get on his feet again, but she surprised him by reaching out and placing her hand on his forearm. His gaze latched on to that point of contact, unsure what it meant.

'Will you stay? I'd like for us to talk about what happens going forward.'

He swallowed and his gaze darted to hers. What was she up to? She stared back at him with those deep blue eyes and her face was a mask of civility. It didn't help that he could smell her, or that his body recognised that scent. He scented her like a hound. She smelled of flowers and leather and his entire body tightened in awareness of her. Particularly after last night when he'd touched that sweet mound between her legs and felt proof of her desire for him. When he'd been so close to making her his.

He'd never negotiated with an enemy he wanted to bed. It had to be a bad idea. Nevertheless, it appeared he had no choice if he wanted to move forward peacefully. Nodding, he eased back down on to the bench.

'Fair enough. What did you have in mind?'

'Last night you said that today we could start anew.' Her voice was soft, but the husky timbre that he enjoyed so much was laced beneath the softness. 'Did you mean that?'

'Aye.' He cleared his throat over the word. He'd actually very much like to forget last night had even happened. It had only whetted his appetite for more of her. The intoxicating scent of her arousal was firmly etched in his mind and he remembered the feel of her silky skin beneath his hand.

She nodded. 'Good, because I'd like that, too. I fear that our strife could overly influence our warriors and we should be working to unite them…not keep them separate.'

He raised an eyebrow and inclined his head in acknowledgement of her words. She spoke the truth about the need to create unity instead of conflict. And he started to relax. She wasn't up to anything after all. Her sudden willingness to compromise and forge ahead was a direct result of the spanking. He couldn't help but smile at her in smug satisfaction and play along with her game. If she wanted to pretend that she'd come to this juncture on her own, then he'd allow her to save face.

Eirik's words came back to him and for the first time they made sense.

'She may want to be a warrior, but she's not. However, you can't win her over by defeating her.'

If Vidar defeated her, if he forced her to become what she wasn't, then he would lose because she would hate him. If he didn't fight at all, if he ignored her and took charge, then she'd defy him and it would eventually create a rift in the warriors. The only choice was to find some way to work with her. He didn't quite know what that way would be, because it seemed that she wanted something he couldn't give her. Independence.

'I'm impressed by your dedication to your people. Did you have a solution to offer?'

'We need to agree to not disagree in front of them,' she said, tucking a lock of hair behind her ear. She'd pulled it back in her usual thick braid and he suddenly longed to see it down around her pale form. 'Warriors need to know that their leaders are united. If we present a united front, then they will follow suit. I understand that there may be some discord from time to time, but if we stick together in facing it, it will go much smoother.'

He picked up his tankard as he mulled over her words. She was absolutely correct in all that she said, but he had the sneaking suspicion that it wouldn't be enough. 'You're right, Wife. But the issue lies in your use of the term leader.'

She stiffened and a flash of anger crossed her features. There was the woman he'd come to enjoy arguing with. 'Are you implying I'm not a leader?'

'You are. You're important to Alvey as its Lady and the warriors will accept you as such.'

'Though I do lead my warriors,' she pointed out.

He inclined his head, conceding the point. 'But it will take much more than me declaring it so for my warriors to accept you as their leader. I'm assuming that's your goal?'

She frowned, her brow furrowing. 'Do you not control them, then?'

He smiled. 'Do you control yours? Do you think if you simply hand them over to my keeping that they'll obey without resentment? Did you not send Rodor to lead them when I travelled to find the rebels?'

Her brow smoothed out as she accepted his words and she gave a little nod. 'I see your point.'

'And there's more.' He set his tankard down and shifted on the bench to face her. 'You are a woman and my men aren't accustomed to obeying women, especially in battle.' She bristled, but he kept talking so she wouldn't interrupt. 'The only way to gain their true respect is to show your worth and gain their respect in battle.'

'Then you must allow me to battle.' She shrugged as if the truth was obvious.

'My wife will not battle.' The words were firm, but he kept anger out of his voice. He didn't want to be her enemy any longer. She'd denied him last night, because she had portrayed him in her mind as her enemy, and she couldn't understand how to give herself to him while keeping him in that slot reserved for her enemy.

He understood it. In that moment of looking down at her, he'd realised much more about her than he ever had before. She didn't see herself as a woman who was meant to submit her own will to his. She saw herself as a warrior. Not only a warrior, but a leader. He'd never expect a leader to move over and let him lead, but that's exactly what he'd expected her to do. And it had been a mistake he wouldn't repeat. He'd have to work with her to slowly have her submit to his will.

She stared up at him. The impassive mask she wore was just starting to crack when she managed to put it back firmly into place. 'Why must I not battle?'

'Because your safety must come before mine. I'm an outsider here. A foreigner and some would say an enemy. *You* are Alvey. The people here know you and respect you and your family. Have you thought of what might become of Alvey if you were to perish? Do you suppose some might consider us Danes intruders? Invaders that need to be pushed out of Alvey?'

Her eyes widened a bit and he realised that she'd

never considered that, or at least never considered that as a negative outcome, so he elaborated. 'If that happens, your men will have to gather support from the farms and perhaps even the tribes from the north. I'll expect that to happen, so I'll send word to Jarl Eirik. He'll send more men to secure the area. Your death could mean war between our people. And the end of the Alvey you love.' He paused for dramatic effect before adding in a lowered voice, 'Deep in your heart, you know that the Danes will win such a war.'

Her lips parted as she drew in a shaky breath. The tip of her pink tongue came out to moisten her bottom lip and the desire he'd only barely kept tamped down flared to life. He wanted to suck that moist bottom lip into his mouth and taste the sweet honey her tongue had left behind. He was lusting after his own wife. This was worse than the time he'd been fifteen and his older brother Gunnar had decided his punishment for not cleaning Gunnar's boat properly should be to not have a woman for a month. He'd paid them all well to keep away from Vidar.

Only his wife should be his by rights. It was her own stubbornness keeping her away from him.

'I'll need to think about what you've said. It's an interesting point that I hadn't considered.' Her gaze jumped to his and then down to his mouth before touching on his shoulders as she looked back to her meal. His misery was made even worse by the knowledge that she wanted him as much as he wanted her. He knew that he couldn't force the issue, but that didn't mean he couldn't keep pushing her.

'Think about it. It's good to see you more compliant this morning. Had I known spanking you would bring you to heel, I'd have done it on our wedding night.'

She gasped as she jerked her head up in outrage. Anger glittered in her eyes and her face mottled with rage. 'How dare you?'

He couldn't help the corner of his mouth from tipping upward. She was beautiful in her anger. 'It's true. And what's more…you liked it.'

She drew her hand back with the intention of slapping him, but tightened it in a fist and dropped it in her lap as she thought better of it. 'I should slap your arrogant face,' she hissed.

'Why? Because then I'd spank you again?'

She glared at him as he rose to his feet. She couldn't deny what had happened between them last night, but neither could she admit to it. It didn't matter. He'd make her admit it with a little time. Giving her a nod, he left to go to the sparring field.

Gwendolyn was so angry that she was shaking. The urge to chase after him nearly moved her to her feet, but what then? What would she say to him? That he was wrong? That he had no right to say those things? That he shouldn't have used her own desire against her?

He had every right to say them, just as he'd had every right to punish her. He was her husband.

She dropped her face into her hands and took a deep breath to beat down the impotent rage building inside her. She'd come down here to attempt to work with him, because after last night…well, it was clear that things couldn't continue as before. If they didn't start to work together, she was afraid of the things he could do. The biggest one being that he could undermine her authority until he eventually made her men disrespect her. She had no choice but to figure out a way to work with him, even if she hated every moment of it.

As her rage gave way to resignation, Gwendolyn took a few moments to eat her meal. She thought of what Vidar had said about her importance to Alvey. She wanted to deny their truth, but she couldn't. A small groan of frustration escaped her. Why couldn't he be a fool? Why did he have to make such good arguments? If something happened to her in battle, she wasn't entirely certain that what he'd predicted wouldn't come to pass. If Jarl Eirik did attack her people…well, the Jarl did command an army of men. It was possible the Danes would win that battle. Even if her people won, there were certain to be casualties. She didn't want that if her actions could result in a peaceful co-existence.

It gave her a new perspective on Vidar banning her from fighting. If only he had presented his argument to her in a clear and articulate manner before he'd banned her outright. Perhaps that's one thing they could work on. She could show him how reasonable she could be when he presented her with logical arguments as opposed to commanding her with unreasonable edicts.

Finished with her meal, she pushed back from the table and worked herself past his now-vacant seat on the bench. She breathed in and his lingering scent filled her nostrils. The unique combination of leather and man caused excitement to flutter in her belly. She pressed a hand to her stomach to ward it off and continued towards the door as if it hadn't happened. She still didn't know how to come to terms with physically wanting him. It would have been so easy for her to give herself over to him. Thank goodness she'd had the presence of mind to resist. She had a sneaking suspicion that once she allowed him total possession of her body, it would be very hard for her to deny him anything.

Heat bloomed over her cheeks as she recalled exactly how good it had felt to have him touch her so intimately. But that was followed by shame. It wasn't the pain of the spanking that had caused her to cry herself to sleep last night. It was the embarrassment of nearly submitting to him and it stung her all over again.

Stepping out into the low morning light, she paused as she took note of the activity in the yard. She half-expected the Danes to notice her immediately and smirk at her. They'd consider it something of a victory that their leader had bested her. But, as she stood there waiting for their judgement and censure, no one seemed to pay her very much attention. Some of them were making their way to the sparring field where she could already hear the shouts and metal clashing as the men practised.

She wanted to head in that direction, but there were more pressing matters this morning. Most of the villagers and farmers had stayed to feast while she and her husband had been away chasing rebels. Now that the rebels had moved on, many of them needed to return home.

Annis called to her and Gwendolyn turned to see that groups of people were beginning to assemble their wagons near the gates. 'I'm glad you decided to stay until the danger had passed,' Gwendolyn said as she hugged her sister. Bending, she scooped up her little nephew and got a smile from him as she tossed him in the air.

'And I'm glad to see that you've come back without injury.' Annis raised a brow as she picked up a satchel and tossed it to Eadward in the wagon.

'Of course I'm without injury.' Gwendolyn rolled her eyes at the dramatics and cuddled the toddler, rubbing her cheek against his soft, curly hair. 'Everyone is behaving as if I've never ridden out chasing criminals before.'

Annis looked suitably chastened as she picked up the last satchel for her husband to load. 'I suppose you're right. I only worry now, because I sup-

pose there was never a chance of you…you know.'
Annis' glance down to Gwendolyn's belly told her
exactly what her sister meant. She was concerned
that Gwendolyn was carrying a child.

'There is still not a chance of that.'

Annis' mouth gaped open and she lowered her
voice. 'What do you mean?'

The toddler tugged the end of Gwendolyn's braid
and promptly put it in his mouth. Gwendolyn smiled
as she tugged it free and gently pinched the tip of
his nose. He giggled and brushed her hand away
as he checked to make sure it was intact. 'I think
you know what that means, dear sister.' Then she
leaned in closer so that Eadward wouldn't over-
hear. 'Women who don't lie with men don't have
babies.' The memory of his touch on her most private place last night pushed its way into her mind
and she blushed.

Annis looked as if she'd just been scandalised. It
was a look Gwendolyn was coming to expect from
her sister. 'He's your husband, Gwendolyn. You
must…do your duty. Alvey needs a child.'

Gwendolyn frowned. She'd much preferred it
when she'd been a warrior and Alvey's protector.
She wasn't enjoying being Alvey's Lady. It came
with too many duties that included too many restric-
tions. Cedric should still be here and his wife should
be the Lady. 'I don't know that to be true. Alvey has
done fine without a child. If it needs a child, then
here…how about little Eadward?' She held up the

child and he squirmed to get down, so she sat him on his feet. He immediately ran to the wagon and tried to climb in to reach his father who was busy settling their supplies.

Annis sighed as if she were growing impatient and put her arm around Gwendolyn's shoulders. 'That's not possible now. You've married and Alvey has a new Lord. Do you suppose Jarl Eirik would allow himself to lose Alvey's influence if something were to happen to you or your husband?'

And they were back to her death again. Everyone seemed unduly preoccupied with her death as if it were imminent. 'Do not, Annis.'

But the plea didn't stop her and she kept on talking as if Gwendolyn hadn't interrupted her. 'A child belonging to both you and Vidar would help to unite us. It would lessen the chance of a rebellion should our people resist Jarl Eirik. It would make everyone safer. It's your duty now to see to the safety of everyone here.'

Gwendolyn shook her head. She didn't want to listen to this right now. Perhaps Annis spoke the truth, but she couldn't listen to it, not so soon after listening to Vidar's lecture on how important her safety had become. Because of this marriage, she wasn't allowed to ride out past the gates without an armed squadron to protect her, apparently, but she also had to commit herself to sharing her husband's bed every night while giving him control of her body.

She ignored the way the thought made the kindling deep in her belly flare to life. She absolutely would not be coming to terms with the curiosity of what it would be like to give up control of herself to Vidar.

'I cannot do that now, Annis. I cannot simply become someone else because of a wedding ceremony.' She couldn't lose sight of who she was. Giving in to Vidar would do exactly that, because he demanded so much of who she was to change. As long as she resisted, then she knew that she would still be the person she knew.

Much to her surprise, Annis gave her a sad smile and squeezed her shoulders. 'It will take some time, but you'll figure out how to become Lady and keep a part of yourself.'

Gwendolyn wasn't so certain of that fact. Nevertheless, she pulled herself together enough to say goodbye to her sister's family, then she made certain to visit each family who was leaving that day, thanking them for making the trip and participating in the feast.

She was very shocked when she looked over as the procession began filing through the gates to see Vidar standing there to speak to each family who passed through. Pulling something out of a drawstring bag, he pressed the tiny trinket into the hand of the man he was speaking with. She frowned and starting walking over to him. Before she reached him, he'd passed out more to two different men who appeared to be the heads of their households.

It was only when she was nearly upon him that she saw him withdraw a small coin that shimmered in the sunlight. He gave her a glance of acknowledgement, but his attention was focused on the people as they left. She stood stiffly beside him, nodding to them all as they passed. When the last of them had filed out of the gate, Gwendolyn said, 'If you're trying to bribe them with coin, I'm not sure how effective you'll be. They may take your coin and still revolt.'

He grinned and she fell in beside him as he walked towards the sparring field. 'Then I suppose I must keep you safe at all cost.' He drew up short, as if he'd just thought of something. 'It strikes me that there is another way to keep your Saxons' allegiance.'

He'd turned to look at her, and she found herself shying away from the intensity of his gaze. After giving her desire for him away, she found that she had trouble looking him in the eye. 'A child?' she asked, Annis's words still fresh in her mind.

'Aye, so you've considered it?'

'The idea has been presented to me.'

He took in a breath through his nose as he looked down at her, but he didn't say anything for a moment. Unwilling to look like a coward, she forced herself to hold his gaze. Finally, he took a step, closing the distance between them, but he didn't touch her. He simply dipped his head and whispered against her hair, 'It would be good between us. After last night, you know that to be true.'

He continued on to the sparring field, leaving her to draw in a shaky breath. Every fire that she'd thought she'd managed to put out flared to life within her. She'd been right. He knew exactly the effect he had on her and he wouldn't let up until he'd won.

'Tomorrow morning,' he called back, turning slightly to look at her as he walked backwards for a bit. For a moment, she had the strange idea that perhaps he was telling her the time of her future submission to him. 'My warriors have expressed an interest in learning more about your crossbow. Meet with the warriors on the sparring field then so that you can demonstrate your archery skills. I'm thinking of having bows made for some of the warriors. They'll need an able teacher.'

He turned and kept walking, leaving her utterly confused, yet hopeful. For the very first time since she'd shot her arrow into that ridiculous masthead on his ship, she thought that perhaps they could find a way to work together.

Chapter Twelve

The woman knew her way around a crossbow. Vidar hadn't doubted that fact after she'd put an arrow in the eye of the lion carved into his ship, but seeing her today drove the point home. She'd spent the past half-hour putting an arrow into every target that his men found for her. It had become something of a spectacle with all of the warriors stopping to watch her put on her performance. Originally, he'd planned to have her train the few who had expressed an interest in learning, but as soon as her feat had gained an audience, he'd been reluctant to put the men back to work. He wanted them to watch her and admire her skill. More and more he was coming to think of her as his and he liked that she was competent in her ability.

He smiled as she let fly her last arrow. It zipped through the air and landed with a thud in the wooden target across the field nearly a hundred paces away. The men were suitably impressed with a few even

cheering her success. Pride for her swelled within
him. He was finding that he was quite happy with
her as his wife. With her ability to hunt down rebels,
retrieve stolen sheep and handle a crossbow. He was
captivated by her. He knew full-grown warriors who
wouldn't be that astute if left to their own devices.
He simply wasn't certain how that all fit with the
role of the person who was supposed to be his wife.

As she held the crossbow out to demonstrate how
it moved to one of his men, Vidar allowed his gaze
to wander down to her bottom. She'd gone to bed
last night before he'd gone upstairs to their chamber.
Though he hadn't expected her to give in to him so
soon, he'd been disappointed to find her sleeping
none the less.

She was finished with her demonstration, so
some of the men began to go back to their previous
occupations. Vidar had planned to take a group out
to the countryside. It was time to start thinking of
establishing farms for some of them since their days
of constant battle were behind them. They'd need
women to marry and help run the farms, and Vidar
planned to go back to Eirik's home in late summer
to bring some back with him. In the meantime, he'd
have to talk to Gwendolyn about some of the unat-
tached women here. It would be good to start inter-
marrying to lessen the divisiveness.

As he approached her, one of his men grabbed
the crossbow from her and sighted it, aiming it at a
sack that had been stuffed with hay and set up as a

target. It wasn't loaded with an arrow. Gwendolyn glared at the man. 'That's my crossbow. I've brought others for you to use.'

A group of around ten of his men had stayed back to learn how the crossbow worked, with the goal of being skilled enough to use it for protection. The man, Ivar, gave her a glance, but didn't make a move to return it to her. He just held it up and sighted it again.

Vidar forced down the anger he felt rising to the surface. 'The crossbow is good craftsmanship?' he asked, stepping up to the group and keeping his voice calm.

Ivar gave him a grin and nodded. 'Aye, very good.' He ran his fingers over the wood engraving. It was a carving of some sort of beast's head. Vidar had never noticed that carving before and thought that he should ask her about it later. He wondered if it had significance to her. There were so many things about her that he didn't know. 'Not like those.' Ivar pointed at the crossbows set on the barrels lined up next to them. They were plain wood and metal with no ornamentation.

'Those are the ones the boys practise with.' Gwendolyn frowned, clearly still unhappy that Ivar held her beloved crossbow.

Vidar nodded. 'That makes sense. We don't allow the boys to practise with full swords either. They have to earn their swords.' She glanced at him, shock widening her eyes, and he wondered if she'd really not expected him to come to her defence. It bothered him that she saw him as an adversary. But with the spanking, how could she not? He really was out of his depth dealing with a wife.

'I'm no boy,' Ivar said. 'I'll not play with a boy's weapon.'

'You're no marksman yet,' Gwendolyn said. 'You'll not get your crossbow until you've earned it.' She pointed to the wooden mark she'd hit at a hundred paces. 'You hit that five times in a row and we'll say that you're ready.'

Vidar smiled, proud that she was strong enough that she hadn't allowed Ivar to cower her. Ivar was an excellent warrior, but he was strong willed and it took a deft hand to keep him in line. She caught Vidar's eye and the hint of a blush stained her cheeks. He very much liked that he made her react that way.

Instead of replying, Ivar grabbed an arrow from the wooden box and notched it in her crossbow. Pulling it up, he sighted it and let the arrow fly. It flew wildly off course, coming to rest in the dirt several yards from its intended target. The men all laughed. Ivar scowled and Gwendolyn gave him a smile as she held out her hand for the crossbow. He shoved it towards her.

'With practice you'll earn your own crossbow, with whatever carving you want,' she assured him.

Ivar grunted and made to walk off, but Vidar grabbed his arm. 'Where are you going?'

'I won't be taught by a woman.'

Vidar silently cursed. This was what he'd been afraid of. He might have agreed with Ivar, but seeing Gwendolyn so blatantly disrespected was infuriating. She'd pulled off a grand feat by tracking the rebels and beating them. If only she hadn't lied to him and disobeyed him in the process. But then she never would have accomplished that feat, because he never would have allowed her to go, he reminded himself. Nevertheless, the act should have earned her some respect from the men. At the very least her demonstration should have garnered her some respect. Ivar was simply being an ass, because he couldn't stand to take instruction from someone he perceived to be weaker.

'Would you rather be taught by a woman or bested by one? Because right now, she's besting you.'

Ivar grimaced.

'Stay,' Vidar urged, though it was a command and not a request. 'You'll learn in time.'

Ivar didn't respond, but he didn't walk away. The other men in the group took the crossbows Gwendolyn gave them and followed her directive to start with the targets she'd had lined up before them.

She caught his eye and tipped her head in thanks. He smiled at her, his gaze straying to her bottom once again as she turned to continue the lesson. Perhaps one day soon, he'd convince her to thank him in bed. He couldn't think of a better place than their bed to work out those aggressions.

* * *

The bristles of the comb massaged her scalp as she dragged it through her hair. Gwendolyn had spent the past few moments getting out all the tangles, so it slid through easily. Her scalp tingled as the comb gently scraped over it, so she closed her eyes and let it relax her. Vidar hadn't returned yet from taking some of his men out looking for farmland, so it was the first time she'd had complete privacy in her chamber since their marriage. Because she'd been so accustomed to having her privacy, sharing the chamber with him was quite an adjustment. She was always worried about him barging in on her.

And yet, even when he wasn't here, he was in her thoughts. She'd been surprised at how he'd encouraged her crossbow lessons with his men. He'd even stepped in with Ivar, who had been close to outright defiance. She wasn't certain how she'd expected Vidar to respond, but it wasn't with support of her. She'd liked it more than she cared to admit, almost as much as she'd liked the way his eyes had admired her accuracy with the crossbow. It had fed her hope. If she could show her husband that she was competent, then it was possible that he'd come to accept her as she was. She could be Lady of Alvey, but she also had to be a warrior of Alvey. It was who she was. If he could come to terms with that…then perhaps there could be more for them.

She glanced over at the bed, remembering what had happened there. Heat prickled over her skin in embarrassment all over again at the thought of his punishment. But it wasn't due merely to the fact that he had spanked her. It was how she'd responded to him. He'd dominated her in a way that had completely gone against everything she thought she understood about herself, but she'd liked it. She'd liked his hand on her bottom even more. That place between her legs became dewy and soft as she thought of his fingers touching her there. What else could have happened had he not put her on the bed? It was a certainty that she'd had no intention of stopping his questing fingers. What would have happened had he kept rubbing? She'd felt almost like a fever had come upon her, as if the pleasure he gave her was building to something, though she had no idea what that might be.

That delicious, twisting pleasure returned now to flicker low in her belly. It tightened her breasts and made them ache. How had she not known that her body could do this earlier? She didn't even know *what* exactly it was doing, except making itself ready for him. Vidar. The mere thought of him made her entire body clench as if it were anticipating him.

She cast a quick glance towards the door and found it still closed. Of course it was still closed. Dropping the comb to her lap, she stared down at her breasts. Her nipples pressed out against the linen of her nightdress. Slowly, as if she might get caught or as if what she did was forbidden, she cupped her full breast in her hand. Her thumb stroked over her nipple, causing it to pucker even more. She gasped at the sensation of the soft fabric moving over the sensitive flesh. Eager to experiment, she untied the string that held the neckline closed so that she could touch her own bare flesh to see if it would feel even better.

She pulled the sides back, her fingers finding her nipple and plucking. A dart of pleasure drove straight to her centre where she ached from remembering Vidar's touch. She wanted to touch herself there to see if she could recreate the feeling he'd given her or if his fingers held a special sort of magic. She had a feeling her touch would pale in comparison to his. Pinching her nipple a bit tighter this time, she shivered in response and a hollow opened up inside her. It felt nice, but she wanted it to be Vidar's fingers on her. She wanted his hard body near hers as he showed her more of the pleasure to be found between them. She wanted his rough voice and his strong hands to guide her. Her free hand moved up her thigh, bringing the nightdress up with it. If she closed her eyes, she could almost imagine that his hands were on her.

The scrape of the latch turning warned her just as the door came open. Her eyes flew open and both hands came to rest in her lap, grasping the comb in a white-knuckled grip. Vidar stood in the frame of the doorway, his broad shoulders filling it nearly from one side to the other. The top half of his hair was pulled back in his customary top knot while the rest hung around his shoulders. Her heart thundered in her chest at how close she'd come to being caught. Or had he caught her? How much had he seen?

He'd stopped and was staring at her. His brilliant blue gaze swept her from the top of her head to her bare toes. One foot was peeking out from beneath her nightdress, but she hadn't been able to arrange it properly when she'd yanked her hand out from under it, leaving the other side exposing her from the knee down. His gaze caught on that bit of exposed limb and lingered. Then it moved up over her hips, going so slowly that she was certain he must be able to see right through her nightdress. When it settled on her breasts, he took in a deep breath, making his nostrils flare as he took a step into the room and closed the door behind him.

She didn't know if it was the power he brought with him, or the strange power he had over her, but the man had presence. When he entered a room, it suddenly seemed small and he became the focal point...at least as far as she was concerned.

'How was your excursion?' She sounded so breathless that she was certain he must know exactly what she'd been doing.

'The sites Rodor showed us will do well.' His eyes were intense as he walked over to her. He didn't bother to offer further explanation and she didn't ask. Belatedly, she thought she should chastise him for barging in without knocking, but he'd never knocked and to say anything now would only be an admission of guilt.

Only when he'd come to a stop before her did she realise that he held the ceremonial tankard. The corner of his mouth ticked up as he brought it to her lips, silently commanding her to drink. She obeyed, all the while puzzling over why exactly it excited her so much to obey his commands in their chamber, while outside of it, she bristled at them.

He was still smiling when she finished, his eyes a bit heavy lidded. Taking his own drink, he set the tankard on the table beside her. His smile wasn't mocking or smug. It actually seemed very admiring.

His reached out and touched her hair. 'I've not seen your hair down since the ceremony. It's beautiful.'

She didn't bother to remind him that it had fallen down during their scuffle before the spanking. She could feel herself blushing, because she didn't quite know how to accept a compliment from him. That heavy-lidded gaze was making her feel warm inside and as if this moment was somehow more intimate than it should be. Instead of addressing it, she asked, 'Why do we need to drink this every night together? Where did the tradition come from?'

He shrugged and his fingertips dropped to the curve of her jaw. She fought not to turn into the warmth of his touch. The pine and leather scent that lingered on his skin was affecting her. It fed the desire coursing through her body so that she had to force herself to pay attention to his words. 'Some say it refers to when men would steal their brides. He'd go to the next village and look until he saw one who caught his eye. Then he'd wait…and watch… until she was alone. He'd take her and hide her away. If no one found them, he'd emerge with her after a month and she'd be his bride by right.'

'That's barbaric,' she said. It was disturbing that as barbaric as it sounded, she was imagining how she and Vidar would be spending that time. She had a suspicion that it would be a very enjoyable month indeed. If they'd met in a different way, would she feel differently about him? He was arrogant and commanding, and she probably wouldn't like him very much at all under any circumstances, she decided. So then why did her body respond to him?

'It is,' he agreed and his fingertips made their way down the curve of her neck. She couldn't help but tilt her head a little to give him better access. 'But if I were such a man and I had come to Alvey, you are the woman I would've taken.'

She shifted, pressing her thighs together to extinguish that ache between them. Her hands tightened around each other to keep from reaching out to him. 'So we drink together to symbolise that?'

He raised a brow as he sank to his haunches before her so that they were at eye level. 'Aye, to celebrate our joining. To celebrate our first month together. It's also said to ensure a healthy child.'

How did everything with him come back to

them in bed together? 'So it's ceremonial then.' She smiled.

He chuckled and took his fingers from her skin, only to reach down and grab the strings that should hold the top of her nightdress together. She hadn't had time to tie it closed and she hadn't noticed how far it had fallen open. She gasped as she looked down to see that the entire tops of her breasts were exposed. Each side was barely held up over her nipples and the hint of the pink of her areolas was revealed. He didn't even try to pretend that he didn't see them as he stared down at her, gently tying the nightdress closed above them. The rougher backs of his fingers brushing the soft skin of her breasts.

'That brings up what I wanted to talk to you about. My warriors will need women soon.'

Her blush deepened and she pushed away from him, but his hands went to her thighs to keep her seated. 'I'm not certain how to help you with that. They will have to manage just like every other warrior.'

He grinned at her. 'The problem is the women seem to be timid of them. And the women from the farms who don't seem to be as afraid still won't approach them. I think perhaps someone has warned them away.'

'Do you...do you mean that your men want wives or...?' She couldn't make herself say the word in front of them.

'Some want wives, others want bedmates.'

'Vidar… I can help them find wives, but I cannot condone…bedmates.'

His fingers tightened on her thighs. 'Do you suppose your warriors have never taken a woman to bed who wasn't his wife?'

It was one thing she'd never spoken to Rodor about when it came to managing the warriors. Perhaps they did. She had no idea.

'They're becoming anxious,' Vidar continued. 'They've been months without women due to our trip. If we don't fix it, they may resort to drastic means.'

Was he becoming anxious? He'd been without a woman just as long as they had. A memory of how aroused he'd been their first morning together flashed through her mind. It made her blush deepen, if that were even possible, but it also made her realise that if she didn't intend to bed him… Was it possible that he might bed someone more willing? On the night of their marriage, she would have welcomed that, but now…now the idea filled her with rage and jealousy.

'Do you mean the barbary you described?' Would they actually steal wives? 'But you said that was legend and it happened in the past?'

He shook his head. 'Nay, I never said it was in the past. Just that it referred to when men would do that.'

Her mouth dropped open in shock. What sort of heathens had her father invited into their home? And why did she want to bed this particular heathen so badly? 'They would steal Saxon women to bed them and force them to become brides? I cannot allow for that to happen, Vidar. Surely you're not saying that you would force some maiden to submit to the demands of a brute?'

He shook his head, but he didn't release her. 'Of course not. But it's a problem we may have to face. To be fair, the only incidents of bridal theft I've seen have been when the bride was willing, but her parents were not. A month away with her chosen mate tends to smooth over things with her parents. If there's a chance of a child, then they'd prefer her to stay with the man, regardless of their initial reluctance on the matter.'

That sounded much more palatable, but also risked causing the rift between the Dane warriors and the Saxons becoming that much deeper. 'Then we need to make certain everyone knows that we support these matches.'

He nodded. 'Agreed. I think the farm land will help. Most of my men are wealthy in their own right, but their wealth won't increase from trade and plunder in Alvey.'

His eyes looked wistful for a moment and she wondered what life he had given up to come to Alvey. 'Perhaps over the next days we can pay visits to the villages and farms.' She rose and this time he let her, rising to his feet and moving back to lean a hip against her table. She paced towards the bed as she planned. 'We can bring a few of the Danes and let the people see that they're not monsters bent on destruction. Perhaps we can even come up with an incentive. For every family that allows a daughter to marry a Dane, they'll receive a token of gratitude. Coin or a few sheep.'

Vidar nodded, but he was frowning. 'That's good, but don't you think the Saxon warriors will feel resentful? They'll already feel as though they're in competition with the Danes. If their own marriages aren't rewarded thusly, it could cause problems.'

She was impressed with his foresight. 'You're right. We should encourage all marriages in the coming months.' When she turned, his gaze was in the general vicinity of her backside. She blushed as she realised that he'd been staring at it while she'd walked away from him. It made her remember how he'd seen her there, naked, and how he'd touched her. She could tell he was remembering it, too, as his gaze slowly worked its way up her body. Everything inside her turned to molten honey. He came towards her and her heart leapt and then fluttered in excitement.

'Excellent suggestion. We'll start tomorrow.'

She was inordinately pleased with his approval and forced herself to calm down. Pleasing him and preening for his approval wasn't something she was interested in pursuing. If he happened to think an idea of hers was valid, then that was wonderful. If not, then she would not care. She refused. 'Thank you.'

He came to a stop before her and touched her hair where it fell at her waist, giving it a gentle tug. Her scalp prickled with pleasure. 'We can work well together, you and I.'

She nodded and chewed her bottom lip, because he was gazing at her mouth as he spoke. Looking down to escape his gaze, her own caught on his fingers as he played with her hair. The dark length of a strand twirled around his thick finger and it was mesmerising to watch. That was one of the fingers that had touched her so intimately. 'I think we'll have to find a way. It will be best for everyone.'

She thought he leaned forward, but it was such a slight movement that she couldn't be certain. He breathed in and she had the distinct feeling that he was smelling her. He seemed to do that a lot and something about it appealed to her, if the way her pulse fluttered wildly was any indication.

'I have to go down and arrange for our trip tomorrow,' he said.

She nodded, still not daring to look up at him.

'Gwendolyn.' He spoke in a near whisper, a husk in his voice and need so plainly evident that her knees felt weak. 'Your body is willing to submit to me now, just as you were the other night.' She closed her eyes, prepared to deny it, but he sucked in a deep breath. 'Will you allow me to give us what we both want? Will you wait up for me?'

He was asking if she would bed him tonight. Her whole body pulsed once as an intense need wound its way through her. God help her, she wanted to say aye. Who would she be if she allowed it to happen? Nay, not simply allow. If it was a question of consent, it would be much simpler. Who would she be if she indulged in the pleasure he was offering her? This man had usurped her authority in her own home and he'd had the audacity to punish her as he would a child. Her. A warrior who had fought for her people. She didn't know the answer to that question.

'Not yet.' It was the only truth she could verbalise to him.

He didn't say anything for a moment. Finally, he removed his hands from her hair, but his hand caressed her hip as he walked past her and out the door.

Chapter Thirteen

The next morning, Gwendolyn dressed the part of the Lady of Alvey. She pulled out one of her favourite long tunics, a moss-green velvet that fell to her feet. Around her waist, she wore a gold link belt her mother had given her for her tenth year. She even wore a hair cloth that concealed much of her hair, though she left the mass to fall down her back. Her mother would be pleased with her, she thought. She'd spent many hours trying to force her youngest out of her trousers.

Gwendolyn had never missed her mother as much as she'd missed her since her wedding. When she'd died during Gwendolyn's twelfth year, Gwendolyn had mourned her, but it was only after she'd made her way into womanhood that she truly felt the loss. She'd never found a use for the womanly things her mother had tried to teach her, but she could certainly use a lesson or two now. Though she'd been the only Lady of Alvey for a short while, she'd always simply been Gwendolyn. Marriage had changed that and she wasn't quite sure what to make of that change. Or her new husband.

As she made her way down the stairs, she found herself looking for him before she'd even stepped foot off the stairs. She'd let him dress and leave before she'd let on that she was awake. She was anxious to see if he liked her transformation. But that wasn't right, she reminded herself. She shouldn't care what he thought of her attire.

It turned out that he wasn't in the hall, so she conferred with Rodor on the arrangements to be made and spent the rest of the early morning helping to prepare for their trip. They'd visit three outlying villages and pass a few farms along the way. Most of her and Vidar's needs would be taken care of by their hosts, but they'd bring extra food for the warriors they took with them.

When her horse had been brought around, she finally saw Vidar. He stood holding the reins and waiting for her. He wore one of his nicer tunics in dark blue. It stretched across his shoulders, emphasising their breadth, and he wore a hide belt just above his narrow hips. His trousers were tucked into knee-high boots. He made a fine figure standing there waiting for her and a tiny part of her was proud that he was hers.

Proof that she was going mad.

'Good morning, Wife.' He smiled at her, but his eyes seemed to know her thoughts.

'Good morning.' But she didn't say anything else and focused on mounting with as little assistance as possible. It was clear that she couldn't keep her head when he touched her. She was certain that he had direct access to her thoughts when he chuckled and walked to his own mount.

They had ridden out in silence and reached the first village in the early afternoon. A messenger had been sent ahead, but the villagers still seemed a bit stunned to see them when they rode through the gates. It was one of the oldest villages on Alvey land and the walls were a mixture of stone and earth that rose high above the small houses inside. The last time she'd come here had been two years ago when she'd visited with her father to deliver the news that three of the village's sons had fallen in the battle that had taken Cedric and Cam. It hadn't changed at all in the ensuing years. It still smelled of wood smoke and damp soil.

Tiny wood-and-plaster houses, half-covered with moss and ivy, lined the inside of the wall. They were surrounding the large building in the middle which was the hall where Scur, the chieftain, lived with his family and his warriors.

The villagers stared at them with uncertainty from the doorways of their huts or from where they paused in their work. The elders were lined up in front of the hall, gazing at them with wary eyes and neutral expressions. 'Good afternoon, Scur.' As a boy came to help her dismount, she greeted them all by name. Vidar came up beside her and they all greeted him with the deference he was due. They were welcomed inside where they ate a meal and spoke with Scur and his men.

Finally, near the end of the meal Gwendolyn broached the subject they had come to discuss. 'We've decided to continue the celebration of our own fortuitous union throughout the summer.'

Scur looked from her to Vidar and back again. His wizened face wrinkled even more as he pondered her statement. 'In what way, Lady Gwendolyn?'

'There will still be battles with the Scots in the north from time to time, but in the meantime, we need food to feed our new warriors. While it's true our own people produce more than our own share, we need farms to help supplement. Some of Vidar's men have indicated that they'd be willing to run the farms, but that means we'll need strong women to work beside them. We'd like to encourage our noble, Saxon maidens to consider the task.'

Scur frowned and glanced to his men, who also appeared to not like the idea. 'What of our own Saxon men?' one of them asked.

Scur shook his head. 'With respect, my lord, you've brought warriors here and it's upset the balance. If our Saxon women take up with your men, there will be none left for our men. What are they to do? They'll be forced to leave us and we can't stand to lose a worker.'

Vidar nodded and his voice was pleasantly smooth and calm when he spoke. 'Aye, Scur, I hear your concern. We are prepared to gift every couple who marries before winter a satchel of coin and few sheep to ease their path in life.' Scur started to speak, but Vidar raised his hand to hold him off. 'And if a marriage results in a girl leaving her village or farm, her family will be paid for the loss of her labour.'

Scur settled back into his seat, temporarily silenced as he weighed that piece of information. Gwendolyn couldn't help but smile at her husband. He carried himself well here. He might think of himself as a warrior, and he was that, but he was also a lord capable of handling his own with grace and fairness. When she'd first met him, she had expected him to come into the villages dictating orders, much as he'd done with her, but she was seeing another side of him that she liked…nay, that she liked *and* respected.

As Scur and his men talked with each other about this new proposal, Vidar caught her gaze. Something must have been different about the way she looked at him, because he tilted his head a little and narrowed his eyes in question as a faint smile played around his mouth.

Finally, Scur turned back to face them. 'What you

suggest is generous, but it doesn't solve the problem of our men being outnumbered.'

'That's true,' Gwendolyn answered him. 'Our Saxons will be outnumbered for a time, yet before he left Jarl Eirik promised to send more men and supplies to us nearer the end of summer. He wanted to give Vidar an opportunity to settle into Alvey and for us to not be overwhelmed with the new warriors. I believe by summer's end, we will have the farms and homes nearing completion. There will also be women in the group. Women who are hoping for a life here.'

'Dane women?' one of the men sneered.

Gwendolyn frowned. She had understood the reluctance to accept a leader from the ranks of what had once been their enemy, but to make war on the women seemed unfair. 'Some Dane, but I believe most will be Saxon.' She looked to Vidar for confirmation.

'Aye, mostly Saxon women from the south, though some of our own women have begun to make the crossing,' he explained.

That same man said, 'Those women will have their children speaking the devil's tongue. We'll be speaking it before you know it.'

'They'll likely speak the Danish tongue along with your common tongue.' Vidar kept his voice neutral and diplomatic as he answered.

Gwendolyn answered as gently as she could, 'The choice of what language they teach their children is exactly that—a choice. However, our lives will continue on as before. Formal business will still be conducted in the common language. All are welcome to our hall and our table where some Danish may be spoken, but the common tongue will be as prevalent as ever.'

'And what language will you teach your own children, Lady Gwendolyn?' Scur raised a brow as he looked at her.

She was struck speechless for a moment. She had no answer readily available because she hadn't considered having children with Vidar. Her husband came to her rescue and covered her hand with his. His fingers tucked beneath where hers rested on the table and gave her palm a gentle stroke with his fingertips. Her gaze flashed to his face, but he was staring at Scur. It was a strange thought, but it was as if his hand had wrapped itself around her heart, holding it gently so that she could feel its warmth in her chest.

'Like most children, their first language will be the one that their mother whispers to them as she holds them to her breast. They'll grow up secure in their Danish and Saxon roots, with a foot in both worlds.' She couldn't take her eyes from him as he spoke. He seemed so passionate and yet calm and certain that she believed that their children would do just that. Even though she had no intention of children with him.

Turning her attention to Scur, she added, 'My father wanted this union because he saw what would happen to our people without it. We must embrace the change upon us so that we can continue to thrive and defeat those who would do us harm. My father was a brave and honourable man.' Most of their heads nodded in agreement. 'We can do no less than honour his wishes and do what is best for our people.'

Vidar gave her hand a squeeze, drawing her attention back to him. His lips tipped up in a faint smile and he inclined his head. 'Thank you,' he mouthed. She realised in that moment that, despite how she had fought against her fate, she very much believed what she had just said.

After that the conversation continued on a much more positive note. No one explicitly said that their daughters would be granted their blessing if she chose a Dane, but their expressions weren't quite as suspicious now. She hoped that meant the people would consider their words and they'd find a peaceful way to incorporate the Danes into life at Alvey. The last thing she wanted was a war that tore her home apart. Would the best way to ensure that be to have children? Simply thinking about it made her blush and she shook off the thought so that she could focus on the conversation before her. There would be time to think about that later. Much later.

The conversation turned towards the new crops that were being planted and then Vidar said that they needed to be on their way. Their next stops were two farms further out that they hoped to visit tomorrow. Tonight would be spent in camp and they needed to put distance behind them before the sun went down. Saying their goodbyes, Vidar helped her to her horse and then mounted his own, leading them out of the village. This time the children ran beside their horses until they reached the forest. Gwendolyn was feeling very optimistic about the future.

She didn't get a chance to talk to Vidar about his thoughts on the visit until they stopped a few hours later. A few warriors had already ridden ahead to find a location for their camp, so there were already fires lighting up the twilight when they'd arrived. Gwendolyn had taken her bedding and set it up beside the large fire in the centre and a boy had settled Vidar's beside hers. She'd almost smiled at how closely the boy had set it to her own, wondering if he'd taken that initiative himself or if his master had ordered it.

It wasn't long before Vidar joined her, bearing two bowls of roasted meat and the familiar ceremonial tankard tucked against his chest and held there with a forearm. She shouldn't be surprised—or strangely touched—that he'd brought it on their trip. Handing a bowl to her, he sat down beside her and placed the tankard between them. The delicious smell of the roasted venison made her stomach grumble in anticipation. 'What are your thoughts about our talk with Scur?' she asked, taking the first bite.

'I'm hopeful he'll see reason.'

'And I am as well. I think he understands the necessity of our working together.'

The corners of his eyes crinkled as he smiled at her. 'And do you understand that, my lady?'

She tried not to smile as she took another bite and chewed it thoughtfully before answering. 'Aye, I consented to my father's will, didn't I?' She glanced at him from the corner of her eye to see him nod, before turning her gaze to the men who were taking care of the horses. They brushed them down with care one after the other before leading them to a corral they'd made in the trees with rope.

'You did,' he said. 'And I admit that when we work together, we make a good team.'

'When we work together.' She repeated his words back to him. 'It would be preferable to work together in all things, wouldn't you say? Rather than picking and choosing.'

He was silent for a moment, the air growing thicker between them. 'Do you refer to your punishment?'

She couldn't tell if he was angry or not and she didn't dare look at him to verify. 'That wasn't working together.'

'It wasn't, but you disobeyed me.'

She couldn't resist looking at him then, hoping that he'd see how he'd left her little choice. 'Because you gave me orders, like a child or one of your warriors.' He opened his mouth to respond, but she continued. 'And yet I am neither of those.'

His mouth snapped shut and he stared at her for so long she was certain that he must be angry. Except he nodded and his voice was low when he spoke. 'You are neither. You are my wife.'

'I'm the leader of Alvey,' she reminded him.

'We are the leaders of Alvey,' he countered.

She nodded. 'Aye, we lead Alvey. But we cannot do that if we are divided.'

He took in a breath and let it out slowly. 'You're right.' Her heart leapt into her throat at his acknowledgement. 'I should have explained to you so you'd understand why I wanted you to stay behind.'

'And you must learn to trust that I have been leading these people for a long time. I know them and I know what they need.'

He nodded, looking down at his bowl, and if she wasn't mistaken he seemed a bit sheepish. 'I was impressed with how you spoke with Scur. I believe that you do know your people and what they need.' Finally he looked up and the light reflected from the fire seemed to bring out the blue of his eyes. 'I was wrong to not give you more credit when I arrived. I'll seek your counsel in the future.'

She couldn't help but smile back at him. For the first time, she felt as if he valued her. It lightened the weight on her chest and made her feel almost giddy. But she wasn't ready to forgive him all of his transgressions just yet. 'And I shall seek yours.'

His eyes narrowed as he seemed to ponder if her comment was meant to provoke him. He still didn't understand that she was not here to submit to his will. He was not a king and she was not one of his subjects.

'We lead together or not at all,' she said.

He gave a nod, his gaze going off across the camp, but she wasn't certain if he was agreeing or simply going along with her to satisfy her for the moment. It would take time for that idea to sink in, perhaps. In the meantime, she wanted to get something settled between them. 'There will be no more spanking.'

The corner of his mouth twitched and a subtle change came over him. The skin around his eyes crinkled and his stare had lost its intensity. He was back to being teasing. 'Even if you ask me nicely?'

Heat flushed her entire body. Of course he'd known that she'd found pleasure in the act and he'd bring it up. The man was as insufferable and as arrogant as they came. But he was also more than that. He'd just agreed to seek her counsel and be more respectful of her position among her people. Infuriating. She'd label him infuriating.

His comment didn't bear a reply so she popped the last chunk of venison into her mouth and rose to take her bowl back to the wagon where their food supplies were kept. She took her time, talking to some of her warriors and even going out of her way to include a few of the Dane warriors in the conversation. The ones who were learning the crossbow with her had already seemed to accept her unorthodox inclusion in their ranks. They spoke with her openly and without reservation, and she was happy for the progress being made.

When she returned to her blankets, Vidar had pulled his even closer and was stretched out waiting for her. Uncertain what he meant—they *were* surrounded by the warriors—she stared at him with suspicion when he patted her blanket. Her pulse speeded up, but she took her place beside him. 'What are you doing?' she asked when he indicated that she should lie down.

'I'm presenting a united front. Isn't that what you wanted?' His voice sounded mildly amused as he tossed her words back at her.

'Aye, but I'm not bedding you here.'

He chuckled and rolled over on to his side to face her. Realising that he was still in his teasing and playful mood, she relaxed a little and laid down.

'Does that mean you will bed me when we're home?' he asked.

She blushed again and wondered how often she would be blushing around him. 'That's not what I meant.' But they were both thinking of how he'd touched her between her legs and how ready she'd been for more than touching. She could tell because of the way his eyes became hooded, and, though she couldn't begin to identify it, something thick and almost tangible moved between them. It pulled them closer to each other.

He surprised her by placing his hand on her hip.

It wasn't threatening or even proprietary. It was simply there and the warmth of it spread throughout her body. 'We worked well together today. I'm proud of that.'

'I'm proud of that, too.' She was surprised by how pleased she'd been with how well the day had gone. 'I have hope that it means good things for the future.'

He smiled and leaned down towards her. Her breath caught in her throat and her heart thundered in her ears as he moved closer. His expression was teasing and she couldn't quite understand what he meant to do because she was quite possibly going daft.

He stopped and she could smell the honeyed mead on his breath as it brushed across her lips. Then he pressed his mouth to hers. It was a soft, yet firm pressure, and it didn't ask for anything. It simply lingered, his lips soft and warm. When he pulled back, he whispered, 'Sleep well.' And then he laid himself down beside her.

She stared up into the sky, her gaze drawing a line between the few stars that had managed to show themselves from behind the clouds. The pounding had shifted from her ears to now encompass her chest and her legs, but especially her hip where he still touched her.

Dear Lord, had the man decided on slow seduction? The idea terrified her, because she knew that she wouldn't stand a chance.

Chapter Fourteen

$\mathcal{O}\!\!\sim\!\!\mathcal{O}$

Vidar spent the next day observing his wife. He noticed that she handled her horse as well as any warrior he'd ever seen. Some of the north-facing hills were still slick with mud from the storms that had passed through and the little bit of sunlight they were granted during the day hadn't had a chance to dry them out. Yet her horse never faltered. She controlled his reins as expertly as someone who'd been manoeuvring in difficult situations for years.

He noticed that the people of Alvey appeared to love her. At both farms they visited that day, as had happened in the village, they were greeted with reservation and distrust by the people. Yet, Gwendolyn was always embraced. He imagined they saw her as some sort of martyr forced to submit to the enemy she had married. He wondered how they would react if they knew it was he who'd been forced to change his approach to his wife.

It never failed that the women came up to welcome her. Then later, when they were all gathered around the table in discussion, the men listened when she spoke. They trusted and respected her.

Vidar came to realise that he had underestimated her when they'd first been married and he was sorry for it. His brothers Eirik and Gunnar had taught him from a young age to take measure of a situation and the people in it, especially his enemies. While he had viewed her as an enemy and a possible threat, he'd failed to give her the respect that was her rightful due. He'd been unfair to her, because she was a woman pretending to be a warrior. Or that's how he'd seen her. He hadn't seen how truly valuable she was to Alvey.

He saw it now.

She was not his enemy. If he could close the chasm between them, then she could very well be his greatest ally as he worked to unite Alvey.

He also noticed something else. Something that he had never even considered throughout the long winter he'd spent lamenting this marriage. He liked her. He liked being in her company, but he didn't quite know what to do with that feeling.

It puzzled him throughout the day. As strange as it was, he didn't know what it meant to like being with her. In a life that had never included a relationship beyond a passing pleasure with a woman, he was uncertain how to proceed with her.

They made camp that night on the outskirts of the last farm they'd visited. He'd noticed that in their group of warriors made up of Saxons and Danes, the Saxons tended to make a circle around her as they rode. When they stopped to join the camp that some warriors had already ridden ahead to make for the evening, a few of the Saxons tripped over themselves to help her dismount and see to her horse. She smiled at them and handed her horse over with thanks as she took her roll of blankets to secure her place for the evening.

Vidar had the sudden and disturbing idea that she might have married one of those warriors had her father not given her to him. They were all strong warriors. Any one of them could have been her pick, had she been in the market for a husband. It was the first time he'd considered the fact that another might hold a place in her esteem. He didn't like the thought and tried to remember if he'd noticed her showing particular affection for any of them. Swinging his leg over to dismount, he recalled that she'd mentioned having a betrothed. The man had been killed in battle, but he'd forgotten the particulars or even how long ago it had been. Had the man been killed alongside her brother?

Handing off the reins to a boy who'd approached him, he said a word of thanks and glanced back to his wife. She'd settled herself on her blankets. The firelight played across her pale features, burnishing them with a subtle glow. He walked to the wagon to retrieve the tankard and fill it from their special cask of mead. They'd had their meal at the farm, so they wouldn't be eating under the stars tonight.

She smiled up at him when he took his place on the blankets that had been arranged beside her, and, accustomed to the routine, she accepted the cup and took a long drink. He couldn't take his gaze from her face and watched the graceful column of her throat as she swallowed. When she finished, she handed it back to him, a puzzled smile on her face. No doubt she was wondering why he was staring and he couldn't even be certain of the answer to that. He only knew that he couldn't bring himself to look away.

'It went well today,' he said to distract from his obsession. Her eyes appeared as dark as midnight in the shadows cast by the fire. They were deep, velvet pools of blue.

'It did. They seemed less resistant than Scur and his village yesterday.'

'Do you suppose it's because they feel less threatened by the warriors?' he asked, genuinely curious about her opinion.

She gave a small nod and drew her knees up to rest her arms on them. 'I suppose. I think it's also because the farms are in need of strong men to work and to marry their girls. The more people to work, the more profitable they become.'

He silently agreed. It appeared their resistance would come from the villages. Setting the tankard between them, he leaned back on an elbow and watched the men preparing for sleep around them. As if they'd come to some silent agreement after last night that Vidar wasn't privy to, the men left a large swathe of empty ground around him and Gwendolyn. He wished it were necessary. Her gentle scent tickled his nose and an answering tug of interest tightened low in his belly.

'Gwendolyn, you mentioned once that you had been betrothed.' He paused, uncertain how he meant to continue that statement. Did he want to know what had happened? Did he want some assurance that she wasn't pining over some lost love?

'Aye, I was betrothed to Rodor's son. His name was Cam and he was meant to take Rodor's place and lead our warriors. He was always a part of my life. He was older than I was, almost the same age as Cedric, my brother. I always knew that I'd marry him.'

He nearly winced at that. If she'd known him that long, surely she'd developed tender feelings for him.

She continued. 'He was my brother's dearest friend, so when I'd follow Cedric around, Cam was always near. Eventually they saw me less as a nuisance and more of an equal.'

'An equal.' He echoed her words.

She turned her head to look at him and nodded. 'Aye, I could best them both in archery and held my own with my sword.'

'Did your brother allow you to ride into battle? Were you there the day he was killed?'

'My father never allowed me to ride knowing that we'd battle. The most I'd ever seen were small skirmishes when we'd be out and come across a few men. Once we'd encountered a small group of the rebels in the north hills. There were only a handful and nearly a score of us. It was barely a skirmish at all and happened by mere accident. But that changed after my brother was killed. He and Rodor were at my side when we tracked the men who killed Cedric and Cam.' She fell quiet for a moment, clearly lost in her thoughts of that day.

It shouldn't matter that she obviously had affection for another man, but it did. He found that he wanted her thoughts as well as her body. 'Come, let us sleep.' He drank the last of the mead and set it aside before lying down. She stretched out on her back beside him.

A moment passed in silence, her gaze on the sky overhead and his on her. Though he feigned trying to sleep, he studied her profile, his gaze lingering on the pillow of her lips.

'Why do you ask about my betrothed?' Her voice was low, creating an intimacy between them. She turned her head to look at him and the power of her gaze tugged at him.

He was jealous of this faceless man who had owned the right to her hand before he had. He was jealous of the soft feelings she might harbour for the man. He wanted to ask if she still mourned, but given that she'd been friends with him, he knew that she must. And that wasn't even really what bothered him. He wanted to know if she loved Cam. If she'd

been heartbroken upon his death. Not simply heartbroken for the loss of a friend, but heartbroken for
the loss of her heart. The loss of her life.

After a moment, he settled on the closest ver-
sion of the truth he knew. 'Because you're a puzzle
to me.'

He could tell that hadn't been the answer she'd
expected, because her brow furrowed and she smiled
a bit. 'And you're a puzzle to me.'

He smiled back at her, enjoying the camarade-
rie they'd found on this journey. Rising up on an
elbow, he leaned forward to get a better look at her.
Thoughts of the kiss he'd given her last night were
in the forefront of his mind. It probably couldn't
even be considered a kiss. It had been a mere brushing of lips and she hadn't responded. But he wanted
her to respond to him as she had that night of the
spanking. She'd been uninhibited as she'd wrapped
her arms around him and opened her mouth to him.
Her submission, even given for just a short time,
had been sweet.

'Will you kiss me again?' he asked. She surprised
him by giving a nod, her head moving only just
enough to convey her consent. He leaned forward,
hearing her take in a sharp breath. When his lips
brushed hers, his hand went to her hip, clenching the
soft, firm flesh. The contrasting needs to comfort
and claim soared through him. He didn't understand
them and swiftly drew back before he could press

for more. She stared up at him, dazed, her lips still parted and moist.

Before he could think better of it, he kissed her again. This time his tongue dipped inside to taste her sweetness. Her fingertips touched his jaw, holding him close, and it was the most rewarding touch she'd given him. It was her submission, freely given. And she kissed him, too. Her tongue brushing against his, sending a shiver of pleasure down to the base of his spine. He pulled back as he felt that need drawing tight within him, making him swell with desire for her.

As he laid on his side facing her, she looked just as stunned as he felt. Something was changing between them and, though he was a hardened warrior, it scared him.

They spent the days and nights of the next sennight visiting the farms and villages of Alvey. Vidar learned many things during that trip and not only about his wife. He learned that the people of Alvey were very similar to the people back home across the sea. They wanted to be treated fairly and their main concern was having a secure future. He also learned that he wasn't nearly as opposed to the idea of Alvey as home as he'd initially been. He smiled at the thought, marvelling at how his perception had changed since arriving such a short time ago. Alvey was certainly coming to feel like home—whether he ended up staying here for any great stretches of time was another matter altogether. He wasn't quite ready to hang up his sword and abandon his search for adventure.

A rush of pride filled his chest as they rode through the gates of their home. The lookout had undoubtedly called out their arrival ahead of time, because the servants of the hall had come out to line up to wait for her—he held no illusions that the reception was for him. Not with the way they were smiling. The Saxon warriors who'd been left behind with Rodor came forward as well.

As had happened every day on their trip, Saxons nearly tripped over each other trying to help her when she brought her horse to a stop in the yard. These were the ones left behind, led by Wulf, a warrior that Vidar had noticed she favoured. She gave them all a smile, but drew Wulf into a discussion with Rodor. Vidar could hear snatches of their conversation as he dismounted. They were discussing what had happened in their absence.

The warriors gathered around them, surrounding her and Rodor and Wulf. A twinge of annoyance tightened Vidar's shoulders. He made his way to them and two of the warriors reluctantly moved over to give him access to his own wife. Yet when she saw him, the corners of her mouth tipped up in a smile that was becoming more familiar and it soothed the unfamiliar jealousy he was feeling just a bit. His instinct was to put his arm around her waist and pull her close to him to claim her in some way in front of them, but he restrained himself. He wasn't a man given to jealousy. She was his and they all knew it. Going out of his way to prove that wasn't necessary.

'Have there been any sightings while we were away?' he asked Rodor. Ever since the large group of rebels had been found, they'd had small patrols of men going out to look for any signs of their return.

Rodor shook his head. 'Nay, we think they've gone south to give the Jarl a bit of trouble. They'll probably head back this way nearer the end of summer.'

Vidar hoped that his brother hadn't come across the rebels on his way home. Not that he doubted his ability to defeat them, but the men would have been weary after their travel. There'd be a higher chance of casualties. 'Is that when you've seen them before? The start and end of winter?'

'Aye, for the past few years they've been consistent. It's how Cedric was able to surprise them. Of course, their numbers surprised us in that battle. They'd grown in size over the course of the winter,' Rodor said, launching into a retelling of that battle.

From the corner of his eye, Vidar noticed Gwendolyn fall off into conversation with Wulf. Wulf had been one of the men who'd ridden with her when she'd disobeyed Vidar and taken out the small band of rebels, making Vidar particularly suspicious of him. Vidar had seen the man wield his sword in practice with skill and efficiency. He was tall with wavy dark hair and a white smile. Vidar supposed he was rather good looking if one were attracted to wavy hair and smiling men. His wife laughed at something Wulf said and the man beamed as if she had just handed him the stars on a platter.

Vidar forced himself to turn his attention back to Rodor, but he couldn't help but hear her laugh again. She had never laughed with him. Not even once over the past few days when things between them had gone smoother. She'd smiled and she'd shared with him the rare story from her childhood, but there was nothing deeper between them yet. Nothing like what she apparently had with Wulf.

Vidar glanced towards them again as they made their way towards the hall, their heads close together as they walked. Jealousy tasted bitter in the back of his throat. He'd never once been jealous over a woman. Not one time in his entire life. But he was so jealous of their relationship that he had to fight to keep from running over there and tearing them apart.

What was happening to him? She was his wife. He had her and had no reason to question her fidelity or his ability to keep her.

But he didn't have her. Not really. Not as he wanted her. His gaze dipped downward to her backside, its perfection obscured beneath the fabric of her dress.

'Simply bed her and get it over with.' Rolfe's voice jerked him out of his study of his wife's bottom.

Vidar turned to see his friend standing beside him. Then he searched left and right for where Rodor had taken himself off to. He hadn't heard the man take his leave and he hadn't even realised they'd finished their conversation.

'He left. It's clear you're distracted by your wife and that poor Wulf is in danger of losing his ballocks,' Rolfe said.

Vidar let out a breath and ran his hand over the back of his neck. He needed to do something before he lost his focus and became even more obsessed with Gwendolyn. The past week with her had changed him somehow. He thought of her all day, even when she was right there with him, and he laid beside her every night as hard as a bloody rock. Rolfe was exactly right in his assessment. 'What makes you think I haven't bedded her yet?'

Rolfe grinned and it was so smug that Vidar longed to rid him of it. Another testament to how far gone he was. 'It's obvious. The men have a bet going.'

'A bet?'

'Most have the end of the month.' His friend nodded. 'Seems they doubt you. I've given you until the end of the week.'

Even his men knew the woman hadn't allowed him to bed her yet. This was madness. He turned and stalked off towards the gates.

'Where are you going?' Rolfe called.

'To the river.' He needed the water to cool him off before he stormed the hall and did something he'd likely regret.

* * *

Twilight had fallen by the time he and the men had returned from their bath in the river. His hair was still damp from the swim, but the cold water had felt good to his tired muscles. All he wanted now was a good night of rest in the bed that was becoming familiar to him. It was much better than sleeping on the ground. Perhaps that was a sign he was getting old and it was time to settle down.

He was smiling to himself as he walked into the hall. It looked as if most of the men had finished their meals. Some of them were gathered around the tables playing dice, while a few had already sought benches pushed to the far edges of the room for sleep. His smile faded when he noticed that his wife was sitting at her usual spot at the table with Wulf sitting in Rodor's place. Rodor was nowhere to be seen. Gwendolyn smiled at something the Saxon said and the man had the gall to laugh. Had they been talking the entire time he'd been gone?

He wanted to go tear the man from his wife's side and growl at him to leave her alone. Apparently, the cold water hadn't calmed his unreasonable jealousy. But a man should know not to spend so much time with another man's wife. Giving Wulf one last long look—not that the man had looked away from Gwendolyn long enough to notice—Vidar strode past the hearth to the cask with their special wedding mead. The tankard Eirik had had made for them wasn't on top as it usually was.

Vidar cursed under his breath, thinking that perhaps it had got lost on the trip. He turned to call for someone to look for it when someone presented it to him.

'Welcome home, my lord. I saw you come in and filled it for you.' A servant girl who looked faintly familiar stood before him, holding the tankard brimming with mead out to him. She was a tiny, fine-boned thing, with wispy curls peeking out from under her cap. But her mouth was wide, with full lips that he found very attractive. He recognised her now as a kitchen servant, though she had never served them at the table. If the warm look she was giving him now was any indication, she would be eager to serve him in other ways.

'Thank you,' he said and wrapped his hand around the cup. She didn't let go, though, and his hand covered hers.

'My name is Maida,' she offered.

He nodded, wary of making further conversation lest she take it as some sort of invitation. He *was* in need of a woman, but his wife was the woman who made his blood boil. Yet, when he made to walk away, he looked up and made eye contact with Gwendolyn. Her gaze took in the scene with him and Maida. Apparently, it looked suggestive, because she scowled, her eyes narrowing much as he was certain his own eyes had when he'd looked at Wulf sitting with her.

'Maida.' He looked back down at the woman and her eyes widened in anticipation. 'How long has Wulf been sitting with my wife?'

She frowned, clearly unhappy that he'd mentioned Gwendolyn. She lifted her shoulder in a shrug, still not letting go of the tankard. 'Since they came in, I suppose. Rodor came in to eat with them, but he left already.'

'Thank you, Maida.' When she didn't move, he gave a pointed look at her hand and she took it back.

'My lord?'

He raised a brow.

'If you've need of anything, you only have to ask.' She offered him a smile as she took her leave.

Countless women had presented him with similar offers over the years and he'd rarely had cause to turn them down. Weeks ago he wouldn't have turned Maida down. She was pretty and seemed eager to please. The problem was that he only wanted his wife.

She was steaming by the time he'd reached her. At some point during his talk with Maida, Wulf had left, so she was alone when he approached. She didn't sit and wait for him, though. She rose and would have stormed off had he not reached out for her arm and stopped her.

'Don't forget our mead.'

'Take your mead and stuff it up—'

He couldn't help but laugh at her fury. If only she knew how jealous he'd been of Wulf. She was a beautiful woman and, now that he appreciated that, he saw plainly how many of the warriors did want her for their own. It was gratifying to know that she was jealous of him as well. 'You seem angry, Wife. Have I displeased you?'

'You…' Though her voice trailed off, her gaze shot back to where he'd been talking to Maida, though the servant was long gone. She also must have realised that to give voice to her anger would be the same as admitting to her jealousy. Pride would be her downfall. Instead of answering him, she crossed her arms.

'Drink, Gwendolyn, then we can retire.' He held the tankard up to her lips.

'Perhaps you'd prefer sleeping in the stables,' she said, her eyes flashing fire.

'Drink.' He kept his voice steady, but he deepened it so that it was clear it was an order. She hesitated, but then she parted her lips and he tilted the cup. His gaze flickered to her throat as she swallowed. He wanted to run his tongue along her flesh there and taste the salt of her skin. The idea of her submission, given so freely, made his blood thicken.

Something quiet and hot passed between them. When she drew back, she wiped her hand over her mouth without breaking his stare. Then before he could say anything, she hurried towards their chamber.

Chapter Fifteen

Gwendolyn had expected Vidar to stay below until long after she'd gone to bed, so she was surprised when she was pulling back the blanket and the door opened. He stood framed in the doorway, his eyes taking in her nightdress. It reminded her of the last night they'd spent together in this room when he'd almost seen her touching herself. She still couldn't believe that she'd done that. Heat rose to her face at the memory and she hurried to get beneath the blanket as if he might somehow figure out what she was thinking.

The movement seemed to break him from his spell and he shut the door behind him. As he walked over to the bed, he shrugged out of his tunic and slung it over the trunk for a servant to pick up in the morning. She couldn't help but notice that his mood had changed. He wasn't smiling any more. In fact, his brow was furrowed and he didn't look over at her again. He was probably angry that he'd been caught flirting with Maida. Good. He should feel some of the anger she felt having to watch that exchange. Maida had always been a good worker, but this wasn't the first time Gwendolyn had caught her flirting with a warrior, though Gwendolyn had never concerned herself with it before. The girl was free to keep company with anyone she wanted. Anyone except Gwendolyn's husband.

Blowing out the candle on her side of the bed, she settled back against the pillows and pulled the blanket up to her chin. He appeared to be ignoring her as he tugged his shirt off over his head and tossed it away. Then he sat down on the edge of the bed to work off his boots. Something about his silence annoyed her. He was behaving as if she was the one in the wrong.

'A pity you didn't take up my offer for the stables.'

'Gwendolyn.' His voice was pitched low as he tossed his boot away. A warning. It only fed her anger.

'Do not talk to me that way. I was not the one—'

'What is between you and Wulf?' he asked. His voice was louder than it had been and when his boot fell with a thud he turned and pinned her with his gaze.

She was so shocked that her mouth fell open. 'What are you talking about?'

'You and Wulf. He was so happy to see you that he didn't leave your side all night. I'm surprised he allowed you to seek your bed alone.'

Vidar was mad to think there was anything like that between her and Wulf, but a tiny part of her preened at the fact that he was jealous. 'Wulf and I have been friends since we were children.'

He grinned, but it was without humour. 'Aye, just as you and your betrothed had known each other as children. That proves nothing, Wife.'

This was getting ridiculous and the tiny glimmer of satisfaction changed to anger. 'What are you accusing me of? If I had any intention of pursuing any sort of relations with Wulf, I'd have done it long before you came here. We are friends. But I don't have to prove anything to you.'

'Don't you? I *am* your husband.'

She rolled her eyes and turned over. 'Goodnight.' This conversation was getting them nowhere and only making her angrier.

'Do not turn away from me,' he said, his voice exasperated.

'You're an ass. I won't entertain a conversation with an ass.'

He laughed. 'You flirt with a man at our table and I'm the ass?'

That was it. She sat upright, the blanket falling to her lap as she turned to face him. 'Blast it all, for the last time, I was not flirting. Wulf is a dear friend and he was confessing to me that he'd asked his sweetheart to marry him.' His face showed surprise and she felt a moment of gratification. 'You are the one who was flirting and do not try to deny it. I saw you with Maida. I saw the way you held her hand with *our* tankard of mead between you.'

Much to her surprise, he didn't look chastened at all. He smiled at her and it was a very smug smile. 'So you *are* jealous.'

She tried to deny it. She *wanted* to deny that he had any power to hurt her. 'It was very distasteful.'

'Distasteful because you were jealous. Because you want me for yourself and can't stand the idea of another having me.' His eyes were so knowing. Of course they were knowing, he'd felt her desire for him.

'Because I am your wife.' It was as close as she could come to admitting the truth to his words.

His grin only widened, and he stood to begin on the lacings of his pants. Her gaze dragged a path down the broad expanse of his chest to the trail of golden hair that disappeared into his trousers. His long fingers moved gracefully over the fastenings. Excitement skipped along her skin, but it was followed by guilt and anger that she would feel that after all he had done to her. After he had only recently flirted with that servant girl. She forced herself to look away.

'I wasn't flirting with the girl, Gwendolyn.' His voice became calmer. 'She approached me and, aye, she did flirt, but I don't want her. I didn't take her up on her offer.'

Perhaps not yet, but she didn't trust that he wouldn't. 'I don't believe you.'

'You'd believe me if you weren't jealous…if you didn't care. But the truth is that you do care. You want me, Wife.' He paused with his hands at the top of his trousers, giving her warning before he pushed them down. She turned her head away so she'd avoid the temptation to look at him. She could feel the blood pounding through her veins as physical interest awakened inside her.

'You're an ass,' she said again.

'Perhaps, but I'm yours and I only want you,' he said as he finished undressing and slipped into bed underneath the blanket.

Something about that felt very good to hear. She tried not to smile even though it tugged at the corners of her mouth. Genuine relief weighted her body as she sank back against the wooden headboard. She knew that he found her desirable, but to hear him say that he preferred her over others was unexpected… and welcomed. And it had never felt as if he was hers, so to have him say that made a surge of possessiveness run through her. She liked the idea of him belonging to her, even as she wasn't sure how to handle belonging to him.

She glanced at him from beneath her lashes to see that he'd settled himself with his back against the headboard with the blanket pooled in his lap. His strong and graceful hands rested on top of it. The shadows cast by the single candle played over the twin muscles of his chest and emphasised the strength of his arms. Shadows and light dipped across the ridges and planes of his stomach.

'And I know you want me.' His voice had lowered. 'I could make you scream so loudly, there'd be no doubt to Maida or anyone else who I want in my bed.'

Her nipples beaded and pleasure began to coil in her belly. She gritted her teeth to stop the whimper that tried to escape her. She had no idea how he'd make her scream, but it sounded like something she wanted to explore. Instead of answering, she flopped down on to her side away from him. But it was too late to stop the visions that played themselves over in her mind. She remembered him stroking that male part of him. In the brief glimpse she'd had the morning after they were married, he'd been hard and thick and something about that had appealed to her in a way she'd never known.

What would it mean to give in to him? How could she keep herself if she did? Would she be the same? Would it mean that he'd won this push and pull for power between them?

He shifted, lying down, and the skin along her back felt extra sensitive, attuned to his every movement. When his fingertips trailed over her thigh and hip, she nearly jumped out of her body. She'd forgotten to pull the blanket up so it was only the fabric of her nightdress between his fingertips and her flesh. His touch nearly singed her through the garment. She didn't want to move away, though. It took every ounce of will she possessed not to move closer to him. Flickers of heat moved over her skin, urging her to seek more of his touch.

'You want me to touch you, Gwendolyn.' He moved closer, so close that the heat from his chest warmed her back and his breath tickled her earlobe. His fingertips continued their slow path upwards, over her waist, which made goosebumps rise on her skin, and up her arm to her shoulder. Then he traced a slow path down her arm and back.

She squeezed her eyes closed, trying to pretend that she didn't want to turn into his arms and have him kiss her. She almost groaned aloud as she remembered his fingers touching her *there* between her legs and how they had made her throb. Her body was aching for his touch now. She wanted to turn into him and place his hand right there between her legs where she ached for him. She'd only had a taste that day and she wanted more. She wanted to know what would have happened had they not stopped.

He must have known how he affected her, because his hand moved over her ribcage to rest just below her breast. He moved in even closer, so that his hardness just barely nudged her bottom. The phantom touch of his thick chest against her back reminded her of how large he was. Surprisingly, she liked feeling small next to him.

'Stop denying it,' he whispered into her ear, sending delicious chills down her neck. 'You want this.' His thumb traced a circle above her belly, dragging the fabric of her clothes over her sensitive skin. He leaned down even more, pressing his face into her hair and drawing in a deep breath. Then he moved his hips, nudging that insistent hardness against her bottom, and she couldn't help but push her hips back into him. A rush of need went through her as they moved together in a subtle rhythm. The throbbing expanded outward from her centre until the entire lower portion of her body became leaden and achy and hot with wanting him.

His breath was at her ear when he spoke again. 'No one has to know. Tomorrow you can pretend you didn't give in. Tomorrow it can be as if it never happened. But tonight…' His teeth scraped her earlobe, shattering every barrier she'd shoved between them as need made her tremble. 'Tonight can be ours.'

'Vidar,' she whispered. It was a plea.

He nuzzled her ear and placed a hot, open-mouthed kiss on her neck. She trembled as heat flared across her skin. He took his hand from her belly to grab hers and she mourned the loss of his touch. She'd wanted him to touch her breast as she'd imagined him doing so many times, but he slowly drew her hand over her hip. Her eyes flew open when she realised his goal moments before he placed her palm against his erection. He covered her fingers with his, showing her how to squeeze him. Eager student that she was, she obeyed his silent commands and wrapped her hand around his impressive thickness, eliciting a satisfying groan from him in response. He felt massive in her hand and hot. An answering flood of warmth moved through that part of her that begged for his possession and she recognised it now as her body readying itself for him.

He left her hand to continue stroking him and moved to untie the laces holding the top of her nightdress together. She bit her lip, certain now that she would finally get what she wanted, but he stopped and whispered into her ear. 'Tell me aye.'

'Aye.' She wasted no time in complying with his request. 'Touch me, Vidar.'

His hand slipped into her nightdress and took her breast into his warm palm, rubbing against her sensitive and aching nipple. She let out a little moan of appreciation and he moved to take the puckered tip between his thumb and forefinger, plucking her gently. She cried out and pressed herself against him, needing more contact or something to ease the throb between her thighs.

He murmured something in his own language, something that sounded impatient or pained, and then he withdrew his hand. 'Wait,' she said, but he grabbed the fabric of her nightdress and began to yank up the skirt. Her heart started pounding in anticipation as she realised his intention. He pulled her thigh to drape her leg over his, opening her up for his touch, and it wasn't but a moment more before his fingers found her. They slid between her lips and found her wet and so tender and swollen that she jumped when he touched her. She grabbed his arm with both of her hands and held him close.

'Shhh...' he soothed her, but his fingers didn't stop moving over her. They caressed in soft circles before darting over that swollen flesh that seemed most sensitive. She moved her hips along with the rhythm and it wasn't long before she realised that she could feel him on both sides. His fingers held her intimately, but his hard shaft pressed against her from behind. It was the single most pleasurable moment of her life. But it wasn't nearly enough to soothe the ache inside her.

And he knew. Before long his fingers slid down, finding her entrance. His long middle finger gently pressed inside her and she clenched around him, begging for more, needing more as he moved in a teasing rhythm. She realised then that she was ready for him. She didn't want his fingers or his teasing. She wanted his hard length to fill her.

'I need you inside me, Vidar.'

Apparently it was the right thing to say, because he let out a groan and cupped his hand, pulling her backwards so that he grinded against her fleshy bottom. His face buried in her neck, he said, 'Tell me again. Tell me you want this.'

She moved restlessly, trying to somehow get closer to the only part of him she knew could give her what she wanted. 'Aye, I want you. I want this. Hurry.'

He removed his hand and grabbed the nightdress,

tugging it upwards so she had to lean up so that he could pull the garment off over her head. She was naked before him in the light of the single candle, but she didn't feel shy. She didn't care. She was too far gone to care about anything but the relentless throbbing of her body and the need to have him possess her.

He came down behind her again, trailing hot kisses over her shoulder and up her neck. When he got to her face, he wrapped his hand in her braid and turned her head so that he could reach her mouth. She opened for him and he invaded her mouth, his tongue ravaging her as if he was claiming ownership of her. And she wanted that. His dominance fired her blood and made her groan in anticipation.

But she wanted him now and pushed back against him. His hot shaft pressed between the soft flesh of her bottom almost where she wanted him. 'Gwendolyn,' he moaned as he pulled his mouth away and she felt a swell of pride that he seemed as impatient as she was.

His hands pushed her forward, guiding her so that she laid flat on her front. Then he moved to his knees over her, drawing her hips up. Her eyes were wide as she waited, barely breathing, for him to do what she wanted. Finally, he moved forward and his thighs were on either side of hers. His fingers spread her open and the tip of his shaft nudged at her entrance, her slick heat causing him to slide away.

'I'm told this may hurt you the first time, but I'll

go carefully.' His voice was so raw and primal that it sent a wave of longing through her.

'It won't hurt,' she assured him. Her voice was so filled with longing that she barely recognised it.

His hand paused on her hip. 'You've done this before?'

'Aye… Only once.'

He didn't move for a moment and she didn't know if he thought that was a bad thing or not, but she really just needed him to do something because she was going to die if he didn't fill her. Finally, he said, 'I'll tread slowly. Tell me if it's too much.' She shuddered in anticipation, squeezing her hands into fists as she waited.

Slowly and with a tenderness that surprised her, he pressed forward. He moved into her inch by slow inch, as large and thick as she'd known he would be. For a moment it felt like he was too much, but she was more than ready for him. He pulled back and pressed forward in slow strokes until he sank into her completely. She sighed as he slid home and clenched around him as pleasure vibrated through her.

He growled something in his own language and leaned over her, his hand wrapped in her braid as he once again pulled her mouth to his. As he took her mouth, he pumped his hips, pulling out just to sink back into her. Waves of pleasure rippled out from where they were joined, reverberating throughout her whole body.

'More,' she whispered when he stopped kissing her, her fingers gripping the pillow beneath her.

He gave a little pump to appease her, but it only made her push back for more. He groaned and reached beneath her to pluck her nipple, somehow causing a dart of pleasure to go straight to where she gripped him. 'Please, more,' she begged.

'Say my name, Gwendolyn,' he whispered against her ear, his fingers busy teasing her breast. 'I want you to know who's inside you.'

'Vidar,' she whispered.

He pulled out almost fully, only to thrust to the hilt inside her. And this time he didn't stop, he took her relentlessly. First in hard, long strokes that quickly became short and deep as if he couldn't get enough. His mouth never left her neck and she reached back to tangle her fingers in his hair to keep him close when his teeth scraped her sensitive flesh. She needed to never stop touching him. She needed him inside her until she couldn't think.

With every thrust the pleasure wound up tighter and tighter within her until every movement had her craving more of him. Only him. Only Vidar, whose hands made her feel so good. Only Vidar, whose voice made her weak inside. Only Vidar, who felt as if he'd been made to fit her. His name fell like a chant from her lips and his thrusts were punctuated by soft grunts against her neck. Then she couldn't take it any longer and the pleasure shattered apart within her. Stars shimmered behind her eyelids and she gripped him tight, convulsing around his length as she cried out her pleasure.

He whispered in his foreign tongue and increased his pace. 'Gwendolyn,' he called out, tightening his hand in her hair until it very nearly hurt, but somehow pain only meant more pleasure. He went rigid, pouring himself into her, before he fell limp above her, gasping for breath as his arm went around her waist and he tucked her against him.

Chapter Sixteen

It took Gwendolyn a long time to catch her breath. Vidar lay behind her, his strong arm around her waist and his heart beating against her back, nearly matching the frantic rhythm of her own. She could hardly believe what had just happened. And it wasn't so much that she couldn't comprehend that she'd given in to him, it was that she couldn't understand what had happened...or how she'd enjoyed it so much.

Nothing had prepared her for the way things had escalated between them. Never once in her entire life had she even suspected the heights of pleasure that Vidar had shown her. Never once had anyone—not even Annis whom she thought would know—suggested that she could come apart at the seams as she had. The omission would have made her angry had she not been floating in the strange but wonderful glow of their joining. The fact that it was Vidar who'd made her feel this way...well, she couldn't even consider that just yet. It was too confusing and took away from the lingering pleasure that tingled along her skin.

He stirred behind her, shifting more to his side to take more of his weight from her, and his hand moved up to gently cup her breast. She smiled at the pleasing sensation of his rough skin against her overly sensitive nipple. If things could simply stay like this for the rest of the night, she would be content.

'Gwendolyn,' he whispered against her hair. 'You—'

She reached up and covered his mouth with her hand. 'Don't speak.'

He grinned against her palm and, in typical fashion, he spoke. 'Why not?'

She didn't want to hear whatever he had to say. There was a slight chance it would enhance her mood, but this was Vidar and there was an even greater chance that he'd only say something to ruin the moment. 'Because you frequently say things that make me angry.' She didn't want to be angry. She wanted to float in the happy place she had found between reality and whatever it was that had happened between them. Because as good as it had felt, it had not been reality. It couldn't have been. It had been too perfect.

His hand tightened on her breast while his other one moved down her belly to find its way between her thighs. Her eyes flew open as he stroked the tender flesh there and a stirring of pleasure flickered to life. 'We can do it again?'

He chuckled and gave her breast one last squeeze before letting her go and rising to his knees. 'Thought you didn't want me to talk?' She rolled on to her back and he grabbed her ankle, gently repositioning her so that he sat on his knees between her legs. His gaze went to rest between her thighs. She might have felt some embarrassment, but she was too busy looking at his growing erection. It rose up towards his belly and glistened from what they had just done.

'You can talk if it's about this,' she said.

His smile widened and his gaze flashed up to hers. He slowly moved over her, his weight coming down to rest on his hands on either side of her. 'What if I told you that I loved being inside you? That I want to be inside you again?'

Aye! She wanted that. Her body pulsed in response to his words. She whimpered instead of talking and he took the sound as consent. Dipping his head, he placed whisper soft kisses over her cheekbone and down to the corner of her mouth. When she turned to meet him fully, craving the brush of his tongue against hers, he kept going, nipping the fleshy part of her chin as he moved down her neck.

'What if I said that I wanted to taste you, to suck you until you beg me to take you again?'

'Aye!' This time she found her voice and arched upward to aid him, instinctively knowing his destination. She'd never considered that a man would put his mouth at a place designed for a babe, but she was content to let him teach her all the things she didn't know.

He laughed, a soft, husky sound that blew across her skin. The flat of his tongue dragged over her nipple followed by the heat of his mouth closing over her. It was as if there were a direct path from his mouth to that part of her that craved him. She buried her fingers in his long hair and held him close as he moved from one breast to the other, unwilling to give him up. His hand went to her leg, hitching it on to his hip before he blindly guided himself to her and pushed inside.

She couldn't help the cry that escaped her lips as he filled her with one thrust. Pleasure vibrated through her, and she transferred her grip to his wide shoulders, trying desperately to get even closer to him. He didn't seem to be in as much of a hurry this time, because he let her nipple go and rose over her, that familiar smile tugging at his lips. He was breathtaking, his eyes intense but teasing at the same time as he looked down at her.

'I knew we'd be good together,' he said.

She tightened her grip on his shoulders. They were good together, both when dealing with the people of the villages and in bed. Especially in bed. He gave a little flex of his hips and she clenched around him, throbbing for more. 'Vidar.'

He shook his head, still smiling down at her, apparently determined to take his time. 'You're beautiful. I'm glad your father made that agreement with my brother. I'm glad you're mine.'

She didn't know how to respond to that. This wasn't the Vidar she had spent her days fighting against. This wasn't the man who'd walked into her life and tried to control it. This man was different. She took his face in her hands and drew him down for a long, slow kiss. He took his time, teasing her lips with his tongue before stroking deep. Only then did some of his urgency return and he pumped his hips once hard, drawing a gasp from her as the power of it reverberated through her. She was gratified to hear his own groan of pleasure.

It was intoxicating to share this longing with him and to know that he was experiencing the same thing. He looked down at her and his eyes were wide in something close to surprise. She touched his cheek, drawing her fingertips over his closely cut beard and into the golden hair that fell forward. He wasn't teasing or arrogant now. She wondered if she was getting a glimpse into him without all of the artifice.

He leaned down again to kiss her, his lips warm and soft against hers as he moved within her. He took her slowly this time, without the desperation of the first time. And it was just as good, but so different, because he held her and she held him. It wasn't about dominance or who was right or any of those things that had come between them. When she came apart she gripped him tightly and he stared down into her eyes until she'd started to float back down to earth. Then he buried his face in her neck and called out her name as he followed her over the edge into that great abyss.

And when they were finished and spent and so tired that Gwendolyn could barely keep her eyes open, he only tightened his arms around her. She smiled at the gesture and tried not to like it. But she did. She really liked being held by him. She held on to him and brushed her cheek against the soft hair of his chest, resting it there so that she could listen to his heart. When he let out a soft snore, she stifled a laugh. Despite what he'd said, she had a feeling that it was going to be very hard for them to pretend this hadn't happened come morning. For now, though, she was content to fall asleep in his arms.

Vidar couldn't look away from his wife. Her hair had come unplaited at some point during their night together and it spread out around her, spilling over her shoulders to play hide and seek with the creamy mounds of her breasts. He leaned forward and gently moved one of the silky strands to the side so that her dark pink nipple could peek through. He knew that he should leave her in peace now that it was morning, but he didn't want to leave her at all. He wanted to stay in bed with her doing more of what they'd done last night.

She had been as unrestrained in his arms as he'd

imagined she could be. Given the way she'd challenged him and how she knew her own mind, he'd suspected that she'd be fiery in bed. His imaginings hadn't come close to the real thing. His Gwendolyn was spectacular.

And she was also a deep sleeper. He'd already dressed and rummaged in his trunk to find the gift that was now lying beside her. Planning to leave it for her to find, he'd sat it in his place in bed, but he'd been unable to leave her. He wanted to give it to her himself and see her reaction.

Leaning forward again, he ran his fingertips along the satiny-smooth skin of her jaw and over her full lips. She sighed and turned into his touch, so he cupped her cheek and bent down to kiss her awake. He couldn't get enough. Last night, he'd meant it when he said that today they'd go back to how things were, but he didn't think he had a hope of not touching her again now that he'd had her.

She responded to his kiss, opening for him and pushing her hand into his hair, picking up where they'd left off last night as they'd fallen asleep.

'Good morning,' he whispered.

She jerked awake as if she'd only just realised it was morning and not the middle of the night. They'd awoken a few times just touching and kissing and he even took her once more in the early morning hours. Or perhaps she'd only thought that she'd conjured the kiss in a dream. Either way, she looked at him with a puzzled expression. 'Vidar.'

He was uncertain of her mood this morning. If she preferred to pretend that the previous night hadn't happened, then he'd only be able to indulge her so far. They could pretend outside their chamber—he had no intentions of indulging his warriors and their wagers—but in their chamber he couldn't. Not touching her wasn't an option for him any longer and he hoped that she felt the same.

'I have a gift for you,' he said, nodding towards the small chest.

She hadn't noticed it, so she looked over at it, sitting up in bed as she did. He greedily took in the sight of her body. She was all lush curves over a frame of lean muscle. She was the perfect combination of soft and firm. He wanted to stroke her silken skin for hours, learning all the places that made her sigh and tremble.

'What is it?'

'Open it.'

She very nearly smiled. The corner of her mouth pulled upward before she managed to quell it. 'But why are you giving it to me?' She looked over at him then, her blue eyes wide and unfathomable. He found himself mesmerised by them, which was a first for him. He'd never found pleasure simply by looking into a woman's eyes.

'It's the *morgengifu*.'

'Isn't that given on the morning after the wedding?' she asked and, realising that she was half-exposed to him, she grabbed the blanket and pulled it up to cover her breasts.

'It's been yours since the morning after our wedding. But we never spent a typical wedding night. I waited because I hoped that one day we would.'

She blushed and looked back over at the chest. 'You seem to hold traditions very close to you.'

He grinned. She was talking about the mead they drank every night. Picking up the small chest, he sat it closer to her. 'Open it.'

The chest itself was walnut and carved with dragons and serpents that symbolically guarded the treasure within. The fastening holding it closed had been dipped in gold. She ran her fingers over it. 'It's beautiful.'

'I chose it with the intention of impressing the daughter of Alvey, along with the Lord of Alvey himself.'

She said, 'I'm impressed.' But he caught a bit of an undertone of sadness in her voice.

'You didn't allow me to finish. I chose it with the intention of impressing someone I hadn't even met. A faceless wife I knew that I'd be bound to for the rest of my life. I'd filled it with gold, because that was what Eirik had said would be acceptable.' She was reluctant to open it, so he reached over and flipped the latch free. He stopped short of lifting the lid for her. 'But then I met you and you became more than a wife to fill the empty space at my side. You intrigued me, and challenged me, and were unlike any other woman I had ever known.'

She met his gaze, but he couldn't tell what she was thinking. He didn't understand why it was suddenly so important to him to know.

'I knew then that I couldn't give it to you as an empty gesture on the first morning of the rest of our lives together. I decided to wait until we'd truly joined. Until I felt that you were my wife in every sense. That began on our trip the past sennight. We worked together to better the future of our people.' His voice lowered as he reached for her hand, which had fallen to the bed. He traced a path over her knuckles, wanting to touch her again. 'And then last night...'

'You mean the last night that can be as if it never happened?' She gave him that smile that challenged him.

He couldn't help but return her smile as he touched her cheek, craving the silk of her skin. When she rubbed herself against his fingers, his heart nearly tripped over itself. She wanted him still and she was so close to admitting it to herself. 'Then last night you gave yourself to me and it was so much more than I'd imagined. And, aye, we can pretend out there...' he tilted his head towards the door '...that it didn't happen. But in here I want us to know that it did.'

She didn't answer him immediately and looked back to the chest instead. When she opened it, she gasped and a surge of pleasure moved through him. She picked up the pieces of jewellery with reverence. He'd filled it with silver and gold chains, amber and ruby broaches, stone bracelets, and strings of pearls. The gold pieces he'd originally included were on the bottom. 'They're beautiful, Vidar.'

Pride filled him, along with a sweet satisfaction at hearing her say his name, which didn't make sense. She'd said his name before, but it was somehow more gratifying to hear it from her lips now. Perhaps because there was no anger behind it. Or perhaps it was because the way she'd cried it out last night was still fresh in his mind. Her eyes lit up as she pulled out the pieces one by one.

He had the strange urge to kiss her, but he held back because there was still a barrier between them and he wasn't certain how to cross it yet. The only thing he was certain of was that he wanted to cross it. Its existence hadn't bothered him before, but tumbling it down was all that he wanted.

This marriage had changed him. His wife had changed him. He didn't know what it meant yet, but he was happy to see where it led.

'I'll see you downstairs,' he said, rising to his feet.

She looked up to watch him go, her face full of questions, but she seemed unable to ask them. He had a feeling she didn't know how to proceed any more than he did.

Chapter Seventeen

Gwendolyn dressed and went downstairs to find that nothing had changed. The hall was a hive of activity as everyone ate their meal and had their conversations. No one gave her a second look. No one sneered at her. No one jumped up and said 'Ah, there goes our fair Lady, the one who gave up her principles for a night of pleasure.' She fought a smile at that last one. No one would say that.

And it *had* been a night of pleasure. She'd wanted nothing more than to lie in bed and re-imagine it for the entire morning. She'd never wasted a morning in bed in her life, but today it had seemed like a grand idea. That's what had motivated her to finally leave her bed. Aye, she'd given in to Vidar last night. For better or for worse, she couldn't change that now, but she would not allow him to change her. Her habit had always been to break her fast and then head out to the sparring field. It would be that way today. And if she was a little tender between her thighs, then she'd simply keep busy to keep from thinking of it.

It wasn't until she'd said a good morning to the table and taken her seat beside the man that she realised it wasn't going to be quite so easy to move on with her day. It was as if the night with him had made her body extra-aware of him. The heat from his body had her yearning to press herself against him. She remembered how good his bare skin had felt sliding against hers. His scent assailed her and she had no choice but to breathe him in. After spending a night covered in his body, tasting the delicious salt of his sweat and breathing his intoxicating sweat directly from his skin, her body recognised him and longed for that closeness again.

Somehow her predicament was made worse by the fact that, other than a brief acknowledgement when she'd sat down, he didn't seem to notice her at all. He continued speaking with Rolfe as if she weren't there. They spoke in their own language so she couldn't even listen in on their conversation to distract herself from him. When her bowl of porridge was sat down before her, she made short work of it, trying to distract herself from him. And when she was finished she rose.

'Where are you going?' he asked, looking at her for the first time since she'd sat down.

'To the sparring field. We've lost a week of practice and I wanted to continue the crossbow training.'

The corner of his mouth tipped upwards, and

though it was subtle, his gaze did a sweep down to her breasts and back again. The blue seemed to warm and she knew he remembered seeing her unclothed beneath him, possibly begging for him to take her. She blushed at the memory, both embarrassed and aroused all over again. She glanced to Rolfe to see if he'd noticed anything, but the man had resumed eating his meal.

'I'm finished. I'll walk with you.'

And that was the moment she knew that no matter what he'd said, somehow last night would not stay in their bedroom. She wasn't even entirely certain that it would contain itself to one night. She shook her head at the thought, too confused to think of that now.

Instead of answering him, she simply nodded and led the way from the hall. The men who were standing parted to let her pass. She was aware of Vidar's large frame behind her, moving gracefully and soundlessly across the floor. He didn't touch her, didn't even walk any closer to her than he normally would. But now he knew just how she'd fit against his chest and how the top of her head would tuck beneath his chin. She knew now how protected she would feel against his thick chest and how his arms would feel wrapped around her. She knew so much more about what it would feel like to truly be his and, heaven help her, she liked it all.

They reached the sparring field before she realised it. A few warriors had already gathered, talking and stretching their muscles in the dim morning sunlight. She'd been too much in her own mind to make note of anyone they passed. If anyone said a greeting, she couldn't remember, and she didn't know if she'd responded. Vidar walked on to the armoury even though she had stopped at the edge of the field.

What was happening to her? How was she allowing this man to affect her so much? She was disappointed that she couldn't simply move on. This hadn't happened the morning after her one time with Cam, but then that night had been so different. Cam had been leaving the next day for battle, so their joining had been tinged with a bittersweet edge. But it also hadn't been in any way like what had happened with Vidar. Cam hadn't kissed her.

She touched her lips, which were still sore from Vidar's. Cam hadn't touched her nearly as intimately as Vidar had. Cam had been grateful when she'd offered herself to him. He'd smiled and pulled her down to sit beside him on the forest floor. The only moment of tenderness had been when he'd brushed her hair back from her face and asked if she was certain. After that it had taken only a few moments of him above her before it was over.

There'd been a little pain and discomfort. Nothing like the pleasure she'd experienced with Vidar. She didn't know how that was possible considering how much she'd cared for Cam.

Vidar came out of the armoury with a sword

slung over his shoulder. He held her crossbow in one hand and a quiver full of arrows in the other. Her heart flipped over at his thoughtfulness. Perhaps their night together had changed something in him as well.

He held the crossbow out to her with the carving on the wood facing up. 'It's a beautiful carving. What is it?'

'It's known as the Pict Beast. Have you heard of it?' she asked, pleased with his interest.

He shook his head. 'I've seen it before. Years ago we were trading in Hedeby and I saw it inscribed on a shield. The merchant said it was a mythical creature of the Picts.'

'Some would say it's not so mythical. The story is that it roams the lakes of the north looking for strong warriors to eat for its dinner. It's how it's managed to live so long. The warriors keep it strong.'

He smiled at that. 'Is that how it ended up on your weapon, Wife? So that you could eat up the warriors you encounter and grow stronger?'

She laughed at that. 'If by growing stronger you mean surviving an attack, then, aye, it makes me stronger.' Tilting her head back, she looked up into his eyes and realised that she liked the teasing and wanted to tell him more about herself. 'My father carved it for me and presented it to me on my eighteenth year. He was proud of my accomplishment.'

Vidar nodded. 'As he should have been.'

A warm current of longing moved through her.

Perhaps her husband could find his way to accepting her after all. 'Do you mean that?' She probably should have let it rest, but she found that she couldn't. She wanted to know how *he* felt about her abilities.

'You're a good marksman. Your superior skill will be a gain for our warriors.'

Our warriors. She tried not to get too hopeful, but it certainly sounded like things had changed between them for the better. There was a part of her that wanted to press him. To point out that he only meant she would benefit the warriors by teaching them and that her skill would never be used in battle. But she didn't. There seemed to be an unspoken truce between them, so she'd take the win and press him later.

Instead, she smiled and offered up a little more about herself to him. 'It's said that my grandmother's grandmother was from a Pict tribe. She was the chieftain's daughter and fought beside him when they faced disputes with outsiders. That's why he chose the Beast for me.'

'Ah.' Vidar's smile widened. 'That explains a lot about you. Something of the warrior is in your blood.' He turned to head off towards the growing group of men who were gathering on the field.

'I suppose. Does that bother you?' she asked before he could walk away to join them, genuinely curious.

'To the contrary. It means we'll make strong children.' He tossed a knowing glance back over his shoulder.

And as he'd meant to happen, she was reminded of how those children would be made and what had happened in their bed last night. Nay, regardless of what he'd claimed, what had happened between them would not stay in their bedroom.

Despite its auspicious start, the morning did not continue smoothly. She led the small group of warriors in their crossbow practice, but Ivar continued to be difficult. The crossbow wasn't a difficult contraption to learn to use, but it did take skill to use it as effectively as possible. He refused to follow her instruction and as a result his aim continued to go wide. It couldn't possibly be his fault though—or so he claimed—so instead of doing the small adjustments she suggested, he broke his crossbow over his thigh and threw it down at her feet. Then he stormed off the field. She resolved not to allow it to bother her and continued her lesson with the others.

They broke just before midday to rest and eat a short meal. Vidar was trying to make up for lost time, so he ordered them all to return to the field in the early afternoon. This time there was no crossbow practice. All of the men had their swords intent on sparring.

'Do you doubt the need for blocking off the squares?' Vidar glanced over at his wife as she walked up to stand beside him. Her sceptical gaze looked out over the Saxons who were getting to their spaces in the makeshift boxes. He was reminded of how she'd challenged him on that first morning and he remembered how it had annoyed him.

'I don't understand it.' Pausing, she let her gaze wander over the men before coming to rest on Vidar. 'But I'm willing to try to understand.'

And that was how he'd progressed so badly with her at the start. He'd tried to make her submit to him by his sheer force of will. He hadn't realised what a prize she was. Submission given that easily wasn't as valuable as the submission he had to earn. He knew that from leading the men. His most prized fighters were the ones to which he'd had to prove himself. Once earned, their loyalty was nearly impossible to lose. He wasn't certain now why he'd thought her loyalty should be different.

'Fair enough. For that, I'll have to demonstrate.'

'I'm certain it'll be fascinating.' She smiled and he couldn't tell if she was being insolent or not. The woman was a puzzle.

Shaking his head, he called out to two of her warriors, Wulf and another man he'd noted to be good with a sword. He'd seen that the warriors here relied less on the axe so he wanted to stick with a weapon they knew well. When they walked over, he directed them to spar without the boxes to contain them.

'Do you see how he's retreating?' He pointed to Wulf who moved back several yards to dodge the blows directed at him.

'Aye. Wouldn't you have him retreat from the blows?' She raised a brow and looked at him sceptically. Rodor had come over to join them and his expression matched hers.

'Northmen don't retreat,' Vidar said. Wulf had regained some ground and started the long journey of regaining more as he ploughed forward. 'It's tiring. The more tired you are, the more likely you are to make mistakes.'

She scoffed at his explanation. 'Northmen don't retreat because they don't want to get tired or because they're stubborn?'

Rodor hid his grin behind his hand.

'Can't it be both?' Vidar indulged her. 'It's not considered winning with honour if you have to retreat to win.'

'Sometimes retreat is the quickest way to victory,' she countered.

Vidar looked over at her, uncertain about what she meant. 'The quickest way to victory is to be efficient with your blows so that you take out your enemy before he can attack you. Superior strength and cunning is necessary for that. You've seen the way your warriors battle. If you'd indulge me, I'll demonstrate with a warrior and you can see the difference. I'll win faster.'

She looked at him from the corner of her eye as she considered his proposition. Finally, she said, 'I'll accept that wager.'

His mind immediately went to all the ways he

could make her pay when he won. None of them involved battle or strategy. All of them involved her in their bed. He'd yet to determine if she planned to attempt to keep a repeat of last night from happening, but he planned to thwart her if she did. They were too good together and things would only get better. If she'd let them.

'What are the stakes?' There must have been something in his voice, because she flushed and met his gaze from beneath her lowered lashes. He loved how quickly she went from fierce warrior to innocent wife. He loved both of those sides of her.

'Lord Vidar! Lady Gwendolyn!' One of the lookouts called to them from the wall, breaking the momentary spell they'd fallen under. The two warriors stopped sparring and everyone turned. 'A warrior comes!'

Vidar and Gwendolyn rushed towards the open gates as one of his warriors rode through. He'd been part of a lookout that had been patrolling the southern border of Alvey for any signs of the rebels. The fact that he'd come back alone meant he had news to share.

Vidar was there to greet him when he brought his horse to an abrupt stop. 'What do you report?' he asked, switching to his language without thinking.

'We found an abandoned camp. They travelled south, but split up into two groups. The rain obliterated their tracks, but it looks like one has continued further to the south safely away from Alvey land.

I came back for more men to help find the other group.' The warrior jumped down from his mount.

Vidar's heartbeat began to slow and return to normal speed. It seemed there was no urgency. Not yet, but it seemed there could be soon. 'That's a good idea.' He'd already left a few men behind to guard the farms, but they had plenty to spare between the Saxons and his own warriors. He started mentally inventorying which warriors would be the best to send.

'What's happening, Vidar?' Gwendolyn stood beside him, her brow furrowed with concern and more than a little impatience that he'd not included her in the conversation.

He quickly recounted what had been said and turned to Rodor and Rolfe who'd joined them. He listed off the names of ten of the warriors he wanted to accompany the rider back out.

'Those are all Danes.' Gwendolyn grasped his arm when he tried to follow Rolfe to the sparring field to collect the warriors.

'Aye.' Vidar nodded and paused to look down at her. Rolfe stopped as well, his gaze going from one to the other.

Something about that set her off. Her eyes blazed with fury and she tightened her grip on his forearm. 'There must be Saxons in the group. If we're to encourage a union, then they have to learn to work together. It's the only way to move forward.'

Part of him was angry that she dared to interfere,

but a larger and more reasonable part of him understood. They must not continue as they had been up to this point. It would eventually put a rift in Alvey that would be very hard to overcome. 'Fine. We'll add five Saxons to the group.'

'Add five? But you were only sending ten. Why not take five Danes away? Do we need to send fifteen men?'

He sighed, the anger in him starting to sizzle and gain momentum. 'We'll add in the Saxons because it's the right way to move forward. You're right, they do need to learn to work together. However, until I'm satisfied with their training, I won't allow the risk to my own men. They'll go as extra swords, or they won't go at all.'

She let go of his arm as if his flesh had burned her and drew herself up to her full height. He nodded to Rolfe, who walked off with Rodor towards the warriors.

'That's not what we discussed.'

He raked a hand through his hair, irritated that she still defied him. 'We never discussed the proportion of Danes to Saxons.'

Shaking her head, she said, 'But we discussed the need to talk things over. You spoke with your man not even caring that I couldn't understand you. And you made the order to send your men without even discussing it with me.'

He cursed under his breath. He hadn't even thought about discussing things with her, because he was so accustomed to making decisions on his own that it had been an intuitive assessment of the situation. 'We lead together or not at all.' He repeated the words they had spoken that night under the stars. 'I remember.'

She still seemed angry despite his concession. She stood with her arms crossed and her narrowed gaze telling him that she'd give him a tongue lashing if she thought it would help.

'Which men do you want to send?' he asked.

After naming off five warriors, she made her way to the armoury and he went to the sparring field to call out her men and get them organised with Rolfe's group.

The group set off within the hour, and most of the warriors had cleared the sparring field of the boxes they'd made. There would be more practice tomorrow.

He'd seen the men off and walked back from the gate to make certain the armoury was locked up for the rest of the afternoon. But he stopped when she came out, her sword in her hand. It was a beautiful piece of work, made for her size, yet still retaining the strength to take down a greater-sized warrior.

'Grab your sword,' she said. Her eyes were still livid and fiery.

A few of the men who were still in the area stopped to watch, eager for his reply. Vidar grumbled internally, but to her he asked, 'Why?' Though he suspected he knew where this was headed.

'If you remember, we were in the middle of a wager. You said you planned to fight one of my warriors.'

He grinned, but his pulse speeded up, sending his blood rushing through his body. 'I'm not going to fight you, if that's what this is about.'

'Why?' She raised an eyebrow and glanced to the nearest group of men who were close enough to hear her every word. 'You said you wanted to fight one of the warriors to prove how your way was superior. I'm one of the warriors.'

'You're my wife.' He bit the words out in an effort to keep his voice down. 'Don't do this here, Gwendolyn.'

'Don't ask you to keep your end of the wager?' She raised her voice and asked, 'Is there anyone here who wouldn't like to see Vidar spar with me?'

'Gwendolyn,' he growled, but it was too late. Others had heard her and started to come over. 'If you remember, we also agreed that any disagreement would be handled in our chamber.'

'This isn't a disagreement. This is you showing me that your way is superior. We can settle it by you proving it.'

He wanted to toss her over his shoulder and take her up their chamber and spank her again. Nay, better yet, he wanted to do it right there. This was her outright challenging his authority. This wasn't about the wager. 'Think carefully of the consequences of what you're suggesting.'

She met his stare and didn't waver. 'I'm ready.'

He reached up and took his sword out of the scabbard on his back. She grinned as if that in itself was some great victory. She had no clue how he'd best her, but she was about to find out. When he won, he'd take her upstairs and spank her again, only this time he wouldn't stop when he felt how she responded to him. This time he'd keep her in bed for the rest of the afternoon.

She got into her stance and gave him a moment before saying, 'Ready?'

His response was to lunge forward, causing her to take a few hasty steps backwards. He purposely didn't lower his sword because his intent wasn't to harm her. He simply wanted her to realise that he was larger and stronger and she was no match for him. However, she didn't back up very far before she met his with a swing of her sword, forcing him to bring his down to block her. He was surprised by the force of her swing and how fast she moved.

It was clear he had the superior strength, but she moved so fast that as soon as he thought he'd effectively blocked her, she made her way around to his unprotected side. He turned just in time to block her again, but that didn't stop her from immediately attempting to bring down another blow. He'd seen her archery skill, but her skill with the sword was nearly as great.

'Give up, Wife. You'll tire before I will.' She was already panting a bit, but then so was he.

She gave a shallow laugh and pulled back to keep space between them, intending to charge him again. 'I wouldn't place your hopes on that.'

He had to admit she was angry enough that she could probably go a long time before tiring. But then so could he. They fought in circles for a bit. She moved so fast he had no choice but to follow her when she ducked his swing and blocked each one. She was impressive and he noticed from the corner of his eye that some of his warriors had stopped watching with humour etched on their faces. They'd started watching with real interest.

She was a true warrior, holding her own. She'd defied the world around her and those who would have seen her never pick up a sword, and she learned how to hold her own against all odds. There was something appealing and awe inspiring about that. As his annoyance and anger started to drain away, he began to notice subtle things about her. The determined look on her face that kept her focused on besting him. The fragile curve of her cheekbone that contributed to the juxtaposition of her personality. The fragility of her features over a core of hardened steel. She was soft and strong, gentle and tough, and about a hundred other things that he couldn't articulate at the moment.

But she was his. That thought rose to the top, encompassing all the others. She was his and he wanted her in his life. He wanted her ruling beside him.

'Do you see now how someone with less strength than their opponent can wage a valiant battle?' she asked, her breath coming out in short huffs.

He did see. She was magnificent. 'Aye. I see, Wife.'

Seizing on a break in her concentration when one of his men slammed the door of the armoury, Vidar tugged her arm and sent her falling back against the wall of the building. He took the advantage and pressed her sword arm out to the side, holding it secure against the wall with his own. His torso held hers to the wall and it was as if simply being pressed against her was all it took for his body to recognise her. He came alive. She was breathing heavy from exertion, her lips parted and all he wanted to do was kiss her. The best part was that she felt the same way. Her pupils were so large he could barely see the sliver of blue and she stared at him with the same naked longing he'd seen on her face last night.

He'd never believed in the emotion he'd seen in some of the men's faces when they left their homes and their women behind. A woman was a woman. There were plenty of them in the world. Like the men, they were all different, but Vidar had never seen a reason to covet just one over all the others. It had seemed an inefficient use of his time and thoughts.

But he'd never met this woman who was his wife.

He coveted her above all others. She stirred something inside him that no one had ever touched. Feelings of protectiveness, affection, admiration and a deep need to have her look upon him with approval and respect, all comingled in a way he couldn't tell which was which or why he even felt that way. He only knew that he wanted her above all others.

'I was wrong,' he said and she blinked in surprise. 'All this time I wanted to tame you so that you'd be under my influence. But I realise now that I don't want to tame you. To tame you would be to extinguish the fire in your eyes and heart. I want to burn with you.'

She gasped and the anger and resistance drained from her features. 'Vidar?' she whispered.

'Will you let me?' It wasn't until she nodded and his body sagged with relief that he realised how much he'd been afraid she wouldn't accept him. He wanted to pull her close, but he was aware they stood in view of all who were watching them. So he stepped back, dropping his sword arm down to his side.

She pushed away from the wall and put her hand into his. He squeezed her fingers. 'Come with me,' she said and gave him a tug.

He ignored the warriors as they made their way to the hall and up the stairs to their chamber. She placed her sword on a shelf as he closed the door behind them and then shrugged out of his scabbard. When he turned to face her again, preparing himself for another discussion about needing to make decisions together, she fisted her hands in his tunic and drew him down for a kiss. He pulled her hips in close to him and she groaned in response, and he knew that she wanted far more than a kiss. He knew that she was ready to accept more with him in their relationship.

Lifting her up, he walked them backwards to drop her down on the bed. She smiled up at him and held out her arms. He was forced to swallow past the sudden ache in his throat as a wave of affection overcame him. As he followed her down, he loved that she was his. He loved that she wanted him. But most of all, he loved that she was Gwendolyn and all that came with her.

Chapter Eighteen

They didn't come down from their chamber that night, and the next morning Gwendolyn found that she didn't care that everyone had known that she'd spent that time in the company of her husband. Her body was tender and sore, and she loved that. Even more, she loved the way Vidar stared at her that morning at breakfast. The men talked around them, but his eyes kept drifting to her. There was a tenderness there that melted her on the inside. They said to her all of the exciting things he'd whispered to her last night. They had work to do today, but she was already anticipating the night ahead.

That morning set the tone for the weeks ahead. They worked together to train the warriors to work as a group. Gwendolyn acknowledged that Vidar had a point in seeing the warriors trained to fight without retreating. The boxes on the ground helped to improve their efficiency and she couldn't fault that. He also acknowledged that there was merit to the skill Rodor had taught her that involved reliance on speed and manoeuvring. In the end, they decided to train them in both methods.

Then he took charge at night. He taught her all the ways they could find pleasure with one another and she was an eager student. As their days settled into a rhythm, the respect grew between them. Some time during those weeks, Gwendolyn had started to see that what she had found with Vidar was developing into something far deeper than mere friendship or mutual respect. She thought that perhaps they'd found love, though she hesitated to call it that. Surely it was too soon to feel that. Her affection for Cam had taken years to develop, but every time she thought that she was reminded of how differently she'd felt about Vidar from the beginning. From anger to jealousy to affection...he had the ability to touch her the way no one had.

After a month of the truce growing between them, they sat one night with their tankard of mead watching a storyteller. They'd already finished the mead from their wedding ceremony, but the tradition had somehow continued. Every night he brought the ceremonial tankard over and they drank together. He hadn't commented on it, but she loved that he did it. The storyteller spoke in the Dane's tongue, but also in her own language so that all could be included. He was entertaining the occupants of the hall with a tale of her husband's exploits.

'Did you really fight off five armed men at the age of ten winters?' she leaned over to ask him, the muscle of his arm flexing under her fingers as he glanced down at her and shrugged.

'Perhaps I was twelve,' he said, wagging his eyebrows at her.

She smiled. 'I feel as if these stories are invented only to portray you in a favourable light.'

'You've caught on to the sole purpose of the *skald*. Shhh…don't ruin it.'

She laughed and his smile widened as if he were inordinately pleased with that. 'Did you really leave your home and go off travelling with your brother at such a young age?'

He nodded. 'My mother had died and my father believed that it was time for me to be a man.'

She frowned and glanced back at the storyteller as she spoke, 'That seems so young.' Her heart broke for the boy who'd been made to become a warrior so young.

'Are you sad?' He tilted her head back so that he could see her face.

'Of course. You were still a boy.'

He smiled and traced a finger along her jaw. 'Don't be. I was proud to go. I thought I was a full-fledged warrior.' He laughed softly to himself. 'I learned quickly that I was not. But my brothers taught me well.'

She nodded, but she still couldn't figure out what sort of father would send his child out into the world like that. Cedric had trained from a young age, but her father would have never sent him to the far reaches of the world at that age. There was so much to learn about this man whom she called husband and she looked forward to discovering him. He kissed her temple and turned his attention back to the storyteller.

She tried to watch, but couldn't focus on the man as she kept imagining a little motherless boy set off on the seas with full-grown warriors. She tightened her grip on his arm and he placed his hand on her thigh, a favourite position for him. 'Would you… would you want that for our child?' What if he did? Would she be able to control the fate of her children with a husband as wilful as Vidar?

He looked down at her and she was nearly overcome by the tenderness in his gaze. 'I find that I like the idea of a child with you more every day.'

Her heart fluttered wildly. Though it had happened unexpectedly over the past weeks, she found that she enjoyed imagining a child with his golden hair. That image had been coming to her more often lately since her courses hadn't come yet. They'd been due a week ago and she'd never missed a month. And she and Vidar had been intimate every night. She wasn't certain how long she needed to wait to be certain that she carried a child and had hoped to talk to Annis before confessing her suspicion to Vidar, but it was difficult to wait. 'You didn't answer.'

His eyes grew solemn as if remembering his own

experience and he gave a shake of his head. 'Nay. Ten years is too young. What do you think?'

Her throat closed with emotion. It was such a simple question, but it calmed so much of her fears at once that she was nearly overwhelmed with it. This consideration was what she'd wanted from the beginning and it seemed that she finally had it.

'Vidar.' She grabbed his hand and held it tight with hers. 'I'm still uncertain…but I think that I might be with child.'

His smiled again and it was softer, more tender than she had seen it before. He tightened his fingers around her and threaded the fingers of his other hand through the hair at the nape of her neck. 'You really think so?' he asked and pulled her close enough that her lips were a hairsbreadth from his.

She nodded. 'I do.'

He kissed her. His lips were warm and soft against hers, filling her whole body with warmth. When he pulled back he was smiling down at her, the room had long since faded into the background. As she stared up into his sky-blue eyes, she knew that what she felt for him was love. As improbable as it seemed, she'd come to love this Dane. She opened her mouth to tell him, but before she could, a commotion from outside the hall drew their attention.

'Lord Vidar!' One of the lookouts rushed inside and all conversation came to a halt. 'Some warriors are coming back from patrol. There's been a rebel sighting and they need more men.'

Vidar was on his feet before the boy finished talking and made his way to the door. Gwendolyn was right behind him and they made their way to the gates which had been closed for the evening, but were being pulled open. Rolfe rode through and vaulted off his horse as soon as he saw them.

'We found the large group of rebels on the other side of the fjord. There are two score at least. Too many for our small group to attack, so we came back for more.'

Wulf had been on his heels and spoke, 'It looks as if they're preparing to attack the village.'

'Scur doesn't have enough warriors to hold off that many for long,' Gwendolyn said, turning to Vidar.

He nodded in agreement. 'But if they haven't crossed the fjord yet, then we have time. It was flooded.'

'They'll have to wait,' she agreed, which is probably why they hadn't attacked yet.

'It did appear as if they were biding their time,' Wulf added. 'They didn't want to march to the south to cross where the river narrowed after it split in two. And they assumed they'd be safe on the other side.'

'That's perfect,' Gwendolyn said. 'It gives us time to get there and head them off. We can fortify the village and attack the rebels.'

Vidar stared at her, but he didn't immediately agree and that bothered her. Instead he said, 'Can you draw a map of the area so that we can plan?'

She smiled. 'My father had maps created. I'll retrieve them.' She ran upstairs to their chamber and shuffled through the scrolls until she found the few that she needed. Tucking them under her arm, she went back downstairs to find the men gathered around the table waiting. It had been cleared of the remnants of their meal, so she spread the first one out. 'Here,' she said, pointing to the village. Rodor took a corner to hold it out flat. 'This is where Scur's village is located.' Then she pointed out the fjord and the rivers that flowed further to the south. 'Here are the rivers Wulf spoke of, but I think the better option is to go to the north. It's marshland up here.' She dragged her finger on the map as she spoke. 'But there's a land bridge you can't see unless you're familiar with the area. If the rebels are camping, then I'm wagering they're unaware of it. It's a rise in the area and we can take a small group across. Though I think we'd risk destroying it if we took all of the men across.'

Vidar's brow furrowed in concentration as he looked it over. 'The river connects to our river right outside.'

She nodded and traced her finger to show where the two connected. She'd been so accustomed to going overland that she hadn't paid attention to the pathways the rivers made. 'You're right.'

'We can use that to travel across. We load our ships with warriors and we'll surprise them,' he said.

'But they're Dane rebels. Wouldn't they be more

prepared for an attack from the river? They'd suspect it,' she said.

Rolfe weighed in with his opinion. 'It's likely. I'm certain our presence here is no secret and they'll know we have ships. But it's the most efficient way to reach them.'

'I agree,' said Vidar. 'We have to go with our strengths.' He looked at her. 'My men aren't accustomed to the marshes. Perhaps in a few years they will be, but now we have to attack with the ships.'

He wasn't wrong, so she didn't argue further as Rodor weighed in, talking about the marshes to the south and how best to approach. Once they'd made a plan about how to approach from the south, she said, 'I can take men to the north, across the bridge. We can attack from both sides and make our assault more effective.'

Vidar immediately shook his head. 'It's too dangerous. You can't take that many men across. Not enough to outnumber them.'

'I know that, but you'll have more than enough coming from the south.'

His lips formed a thin line and he looked to Rolfe and the other men who had gathered around the map. Gently taking her arm, he led her off to the side, leaving them to their discussion. 'It's too dangerous, Gwendolyn,' he said, his eyes entreating her to listen. 'That sort of manoeuvre is risky. What if we're delayed? What if we don't attack at the same time you do?'

'Simple. We cross and wait for you to attack first. It's not that difficult.'

But he still shook his head. 'It's too risky. They could see you and attack first. You'd be outnumbered and wouldn't stand a chance, regardless of your skill.'

She narrowed her eyes at him, starting to suspect that this was more about her than the plan. 'They won't attack first because they won't see us. We'll hide in the trees, same as we did when we chased the small band of rebels who'd stolen the sheep.'

He stared back at her and became still. She could feel his regret before he even spoke. 'I can't risk you, Gwendolyn. I'm sorry.'

'So this isn't about the plan. This is about me?'

He took her hand and pulled her in, putting his head close to hers. 'My rule still stands. You're my wife. I cannot see you go off to battle. Besides...' He placed his hand on her hip so the heel pressed to her belly. 'You could be carrying the future of Alvey...our future.'

'But you're my husband. I have to see you go to battle.'

He nodded. 'I know, but I'm not Alvey. Not like you are. You need to stay well and unharmed for the future of our people.' He paused and then added, 'For my future. I need you to be well, Wife.' His eyes held a hint of desperation.

She closed her eyes as she remembered his argument for keeping her safe. The worst part was that she couldn't argue against it. It was too soon for her people to have accepted Vidar and his men completely. What if something happened to her and they did revolt? 'That's not fair.'

He surprised her by taking her face between his hands and lifted it so that she met his gaze. 'It's not fair, but I'll do whatever it takes to keep you safe.'

'And what about you? What if something happens to you? What am I to do?'

'I'll come back to you. I promise.' He kissed her in front of everyone and she didn't care that they saw. Putting her arms around his shoulders, she held him close until he pulled away. 'Come help me plan the attack.' She nodded and he took her hand and led her back to the men.

'At least allow Rodor to lead the men through the marshes,' she said.

Vidar looked up at the man and Rodor nodded. 'I know the marshes well. I'd be honoured to lead the men through.'

Vidar still hesitated. 'It could be risky. My hesitation is that we've not battled together before. It's risky if we don't act together.'

Gwendolyn said, 'Then he won't attack from the north. He can hold the marsh and wait in case they flee that way. If he and his men hide then they can take out the rebels as they run.'

Vidar's face lit up and he smiled. 'Excellent solution. It makes sense and it wouldn't be much of a risk.'

She smiled back at him. 'If it's not risky does that mean that I can—?'

'Nay.' He cut off that sentence before she could finish it. 'You must stay here. Your life is too valuable.'

She frowned and he squeezed her hand as he turned his attention back to the map. He made sure that Rolfe and the other leaders under his command understood the area before moving on to discuss strategy.

In less than an hour they were outside saying goodbye, as men rushed supplies and weapons to the ships in the river below Alvey. She couldn't believe that only weeks ago she'd been dreading see his boat appear in that river. Now, she dreaded seeing it go.

He put his arms around her and brought his mouth down on hers. It was a long slow kiss that made her knees weaken as everything inside her turned to molten honey. He tasted like the mead they shared every night and she knew that she'd miss that taste on his lips until he came back. How had everything changed so fast?

'Don't look so worried. I'll come back,' he whispered.

'I know. I feel… I lost Cam this way and I can't help but remember that I'd sent him off knowing full well that he'd come back to me.'

His arms tightened around her and he buried his

face in her hair. 'I'm sorry you have to relive that. But I will come back.'

She nodded and pressed her cheek to his shoulder. 'I know.' To be honest, she felt guilty as well. She'd mourned Cam, but she hadn't felt like this when she'd sent him off. 'This is different. It feels like I'm tearing a part of myself out to send along with you.'

He drew back just enough to look down at her. His eyes were full of questions. 'Do you mean you didn't feel that way…before? Is that how it's different?'

'Aye… I don't know why. I feel guilty. Perhaps I didn't care enough…perhaps I didn't…'

'Shhh… Don't, Gwendolyn. I've never felt this way either. I look at you and I see part of myself.' He laughed. 'It sounds ridiculous when I say it aloud.' He even lowered his voice as if the men near them might hear. 'I've never mourned the loss of a woman and especially not a woman I knew that I would see again soon, but I mourn the loss of your warmth next to me for even one day. I mourn that I won't hear the sweet sound of your laughter, a sound I've only just discovered.'

Her heart beat faster at his words and she raised up and kissed him again. 'Then we can be ridiculous together when you return.'

'When I come back, I won't allow you out of bed for at least a day.' His grin was wicked and it made her stomach clench in pleasurable anticipation.

'Promise?'

'Perhaps you'll consider being naughty while I'm gone and give me reason to spank you.' He raised a brow.

She couldn't help but flush, because his suggestion was too close to the truth of her intention. Also, because part of her was relishing the prospect of another spanking. He gave her one last squeeze before he let her go to board his ship. She watched as they set off down the river, the dim moonlight barely lighting their way. Her heart twisted in her chest.

The grey mist of dawn hung down from the trees as Vidar and his men made their way to the rebel encampment. They'd left the ships further away with the thought that the waterway would be watched more diligently than the land. It turned out they were right, because they'd encountered surprisingly little resistance. A few rebels had been guarding the camp from the south, but they'd been easily dispatched.

He stood in the eerie silence of the rising sun, waiting for there to be enough light to guide them, and watched the camp come to life. A man tended the fire in the centre of the group, adding wood to start preparing the morning meal. Very soon, another fire flared to life on the north side, casting a bit of light across the camp.

There appeared to be nearly fifty men. From their clothing, he could tell that they were Danes. Eirik commanded all the Danes in Northumbria and these were not his men. They were definitely a part of the rebel group that Magnus and Eirik had fought in the autumn. At the time, it had been assumed that the battle had killed most of them. No one had suspected that so many of them had fled north.

Another fire sprang to life and Vidar gave the signal to his men. They moved forward as quietly as they could, hoping to catch most of the rebels still sleeping. Only when they'd reached the perimeter of the clearing did Vidar sound the battle cry and they attacked. The rebels were caught off guard so that the first few they encountered hadn't even roused completely from their slumber. They were all battle trained and slept with their weapons, so it only took a moment for the rest to gain their senses and grab their swords and axes. But none of them had shields and that gave them a disadvantage.

Faster than Vidar had anticipated, he'd worked his way through to the camp's far side. He'd sent a group of warriors to attack from that direction and he met them with only a handful of rebel warriors between them. So when a few of the cowards attempted to flee, Vidar smiled as he followed them on foot. 'To the north!' he called back over his shoulder and he was rewarded with a horn blow. It was the signal to Rodor and his men waiting in the marsh that rebels headed in their direction.

The rebels moved faster than expected, forcing Vidar to break out into a run. The trees were heavier the further he moved from the camp. Rolfe and the small band of men who fought next to Vidar followed behind. It wasn't long before he couldn't see the enemy tracks clearly as the ground became softer and began to suck at his boots, leaving puddles of murky water behind that quickly blended together. A crack that sounded like a branch breaking came from somewhere off to the right and Vidar pointed towards the sound while making eye contact with his men. Giving a signal, he directed three of them to go in that direction.

Then he moved forward with only one warrior, Gaute, at his back. He held his sword before him as the foliage became harsher and was forced to whack his way through. He'd almost decided to turn back, thinking that the rebels must have gone another way, since the foliage was so thick and there was no sign of their passing through. He stopped when the sound of muffled voices reached him. It came through the trees just ahead.

Making eye contact with his warrior, Vidar directed him to one side, while Vidar went to the other. It was best to split up so that they could catch the men from both sides. From the sound of the voices, it seemed that only two men were hiding, but he couldn't be certain. He despised that they were walking into what amounted to a blind. Between the thick foliage and trees they weren't able to see past, he knew they needed to tread carefully.

He couldn't help but wince at the sound his boots made slogging through the marsh, but he tried to keep his steps as quiet as possible. The stagnant smell of the water rose around him as he backed himself up to a tree. He counted the paces off in his mind until he was fairly certain that his warrior had reached the other side. Only then did he hold his sword up high and attack, swinging around the tree so fast he caught the men on the other side off guard. They jumped back in surprise and for a moment Vidar knew that he would be victorious. He brought his sword down, taking out the first of the rebels.

He advanced on the second one, but from the corner of his eye, he saw other rebels pour into the clearing. There were too many to count and before he realised what was happening, he sank down to the ground. Pain blurred his vision and his chest grew heavy, squeezing the air from his lungs. He didn't understand why he couldn't see clearly and he tried to get to his feet, but blackness swirled around his vision. One of the rebels loomed over him. The man grinned, revealing teeth with horizontal grooves blackened out across the front ones. It was the last sight he saw clearly as grey faded in around his vision and the world swayed precariously.

Chapter Nineteen

***

'Lady Gwendolyn!' Rodor's voice rose in surprise when he saw her before he remembered that they were supposed to be quiet and clapped his mouth shut. The ten warriors with him crouched in the low branches of the trees so they wouldn't have to keep their boots in the marsh while they waited for the signal; but at Rodor's call, they jumped to their feet and turned towards her ready to battle whatever came their way.

She smiled and they stood down, their expressions as confused as Rodor's. Gwendolyn had tied her horse near the edge of the forest and had continued on foot across the land bridge that led deeper into the marsh. The horse was too heavy to easily traverse the soggy terrain and not get stuck in the mud. She couldn't help but grimace as she stepped further into the bog and the mud sucked at her boots. The sensation didn't have the same allure as it had when she'd run through these marshes as a child.

She waited to speak until she'd come up in front of Rodor so that her voice wouldn't travel very far. 'I followed you,' she declared as if there had been any doubt.

Rodor only shook his head. 'You have not done well in this. You—'

'I know, Rodor, but I couldn't stay behind. I'll stay out of any battle. I only came to lend whatever support might be needed.' When Rodor looked sceptical, she added, 'From afar', and held up her crossbow.

'I cannot allow this. If Lord Vidar…it could be disastrous.'

The low wail of a horn sounded from far to the south through the forest. It was the signal Vidar and Rodor had decided on. He'd only have his man blow the horn after the attack had begun and only if it appeared that the rebels were fleeing north.

'They're coming.' Every muscle in Gwendolyn's body tensed for battle. She hadn't realised that she'd made a move forward until Rodor grabbed her arm.

'Nay. Go back to your horse. Wait there.' Rodor said.

She bristled at the order, even if Rodor had taken the place of her father and was prone to being outspoken with her. 'You know I won't be in your way, Rodor.'

He nodded. 'I know, but you must go. What if Vidar sees you and he's distracted?'

'And what if he has need of my crossbow?'

'You'll have to take that up with him. But at this moment, you're slowing us down,' he said.

She couldn't argue with that and fumed inside that she was being tethered in such a way. 'Go.' She nodded and waved them all forward. 'Go. I'll go back and wait with my mount.'

Rodor gave her a final glance, before turning and running after the men into the woods. She sighed and made her way back to her horse. The ground beneath her solidified as she found her way back to the land bridge. She scraped the bottom of her boots on the long grass in an attempt to get all the mud off. The battle was too far away for her to hear anything, but the air seemed to crackle with the tension. Even her body was tense, waiting for a signal to spring into action against the enemy, but that signal would never come. Damn and blast. She was still trying without very much success to figure out her new life. It seemed that everything she'd ever thought she'd be was suddenly wrong.

A cry drew her gaze back to where Rodor and the men had disappeared into the forest. She scanned the trees, but didn't see anything. The sound had likely been from much deeper inside. She hadn't even been able to tell if it was a cry of pain, or maybe even victory. What if Vidar was injured? Her heart speeded up, but she forced herself to not think about that. He was a seasoned warrior and would be fine. They'd get home tonight and go straight to bed where they'd sleep in each other's arms as they had the past weeks. She wouldn't imagine it any other way. It was fast becoming that the only time she was certain of who she was in her new life was when she was in bed with him. Nay, when she was alone with him, she amended. Even their quiet talks at the table in the hall helped her feel appreciated and as if she belonged.

When she reached her horse, she mounted him, but she couldn't bring herself to leave. She was far enough out of the way here that the battle wouldn't find her and she'd be fine. And when it was over she'd be able to make certain that Vidar was unharmed even sooner. He'd be angry either way when he found out that she'd disobeyed him, but at least she could be of some use by staying.

Another cry filtered through the trees. This one was closer, but still far enough away that there wasn't an immediate chance of discovery. Just to be certain, she gathered the reins tight and moved off further into the trees. As soon as she settled herself out of sight, it became apparent the sounds were coming closer. There was another yell and it was followed by the sounds of voices. Her heart beat in her ears as she waited. It wasn't but a moment and their voices—foreign voices—became distinctive and were accompanied by the sounds of branches rustling and the sucking and sloshing of the mud as the men moved through it.

Leading her horse even deeper to hide him, she tied his reins to a branch, and she climbed a tree as fast as she could, scampering up despite the wet bark. Shrugging out of the strap attached to her crossbow, she slowly pulled an arrow from her quiver and notched it. Raising it, she made sure she was in position before the men came crashing through the trees. There were five of them. They spoke, but she couldn't understand them. The last one held a length of rope wrapped around his forearm. He gave it a vicious tug and a man came staggering out of the trees. He was tall and wide and his wrists were bound before him and tied to the rope. A cloth of some kind had been secured over his head, obscuring his face, but even from this distance she could tell that blood was seeping through the cloth from a wound near the top of his head.

He staggered as if injured, and her breath caught in her lungs. It was Vidar. Even though she couldn't see his face, and though his walk had changed, she knew the way he moved. She knew the breadth of his shoulders. What she didn't know was how badly he was injured. A dangerous mixture of anger and fear and despair moved through her.

What would she do if she lost him now? She'd only just begun to realise she loved him. What if she never saw his face again? What if he never— Nay! She forced herself to take a deep breath and focus on the men before her. She would not think about losing him now. Not when she still had a chance to save him. What if it was too late? She shook her head to deny the thought and squared her shoulders as she focused on the situation at hand. This moment was all that she could control.

Very slowly so that she wouldn't draw attention, she aimed the crossbow and waited for the perfect shot. She needed to take out the man closest to Vidar first because he posed the most immediate threat to Vidar's safety. However, she couldn't do it when there was a risk of hitting Vidar instead.

Her heart lurched when Vidar tripped, falling forward on to the grounds and landing on his shoulder. His weight nearly pulled down the man who held his tether. The rebel turned and kicked Vidar in the ribs. Vidar groaned and the man knelt down and dragged the cloth off Vidar's head. He yelled at him and Gwendolyn tried not to flinch. She was too angry and needed to calm down.

It took some effort, but the rebel was able to push Vidar up so that he sat resting with his back to the trunk of a tree. She could see then that Vidar had a gash over the left side of his forehead, though she couldn't tell how deep it was, it didn't seem to be gushing blood. The others gathered around him, looking down as if to verify his injury. Gwendolyn glanced over their heads in the direction they had come, but she didn't see anyone following them. Not rebels or their own warriors. She wondered what had happened, but couldn't allow herself to think about it right now. She turned her attention back to the small group before her and waited for them to move away from Vidar. The last thing she wanted was to shoot one and have the others lash out at Vidar.

The men straightened and stood around him, seeming to discuss what to do next. There was a disagreement as one pointed back the way they had come and another shook his head and loudly yelled something. She was almost certain he was saying that they needed to hurry. Once again she looked back the way they had come and didn't see anyone. Finally, the one with the rope bent down and hoisted Vidar to his feet. Vidar pulled away, but his strength seemed to have been compromised by the blow. The rebel put his shoulder under Vidar and helped him forward. The rest of the men fell into line behind and they continued on their trek north.

They were now in the perfect position. She took out the four arrows she would need to reload with and set them next to her so that they were ready. Tightening her grip on the crossbow, she raised it and let the first arrow fly. She had to modify her original plan to take out the one closest to Vidar, so that she wouldn't miss her opportunity to lessen their numbers. The arrow moved almost soundlessly through the air and hit the last man in the line. By the time he cried out, she'd already loaded another arrow and let it fly to the man before him. She was able to take three of them before the other two darted towards the nearest trees. The rebel who had been holding Vidar let him drop in his haste to get to cover.

Vidar rolled over and pushed himself up, his eyes squinted as he struggled to find her position in the trees. She notched another arrow and let it fly, but she couldn't get a good shot at the rebel nearest her and the arrow landed in the trunk of the tree. She caught a flash of movement as he ran through the forest followed by his friend, abandoning Vidar.

'Gwendolyn!' Rodor's voice entered the fray as he ran into the small clearing. He and a few warriors returned, perhaps lured by the noise.

'That way!' Gwendolyn jumped to the ground and ran out from the cover of the tree's limbs, pointing in the direction the rebels had run. 'There are two of the rebels.'

Rodor and his men changed course to go after them. She kept an eye on the retreating men as she made her way to Vidar.

'What are you doing here? You could be killed!' Vidar clumsily got to his feet with his hands still bound before him and hurried to her.

'Come.' She grabbed his arm and pulled him to where she'd hid her horse lest more of the rebels find them. 'How badly are you hurt?' She looked him over as she felt for the knife she'd strapped to her boot and started to saw through his bindings.

'Why are you here?' he asked, refusing to be distracted. 'I told you to stay home. Gwendolyn, do you not realise the danger?'

'Of course I realise the danger,' she said in exasperation. 'Didn't I just save your life? Didn't I just kill three men to save you? I do realise the danger.'

The ropes fell free and he grabbed her and held her tight against him, his face buried in her hair. She hadn't realised she was shaking until she brought her arms up to hold him. He cursed in a low voice and his fists tightened in her tunic. 'If something were to happen to you... By the gods, Wife, what have you done?'

She shoved away from him to see his face. 'I love you, Vidar. I couldn't allow you to go off and not be nearby.'

His brow furrowed and he looked down at her as if he were puzzled. Then his hand came up to her cheek, the pad of his thumb brushing across her bottom lip. 'You love me?'

'Aye. I don't want to live without you. I'm consumed by you. I think that's what that means.'

He smiled and placed a kiss to her forehead. 'It's the same for me.' He took in a deep breath and his hands tightened around her almost desperately. 'It's the same for me,' he repeated.

'Lord Vidar!' Rodor hurried back and came to a stop next to them. 'Forgive me,' he said when he realised that he'd interrupted them. Vidar nodded for him to continue. 'The two have been dispatched. Were there more?'

Vidar pointed towards the three she had already killed. 'Only those.'

Rodor visibly relaxed. 'Then that does it. Rolfe says that we've caught them all.'

'What of Gaute, the warrior who was with me? Do you know if he lives?' Vidar asked.

'We've suffered some wounded, but only three men have fallen.' Rodor listed off the names, but Gaute was not one of them.

'Many thanks, Rodor,' Vidar said. 'I'll be along in a moment to help.'

'Nay, you will not.' Gwendolyn shook her head. She pressed him against a branch at his back and drew his head down to inspect the wound. The gash didn't look particularly deep, despite the amount of blood that ran down his face. 'Are you hurt any-where else?'

'Aye, my ribs. I think I've cracked one.'

She remembered how he'd favoured one side as he'd walked and figured that he was probably right. 'You're wounded and I'm taking you home. Rodor, go tell Wulf to gather his men and they'll accompany us back. Everyone else can stay behind and take care of the mess.'

Vidar started to speak, but she covered his mouth, already weary of his refusal. He could barely stand as it was. He would not be out cleaning up the car-nage in his condition. Rodor gave one glance to Vidar, decided against arguing with her, and left to go do her bidding.

When Rodor left, she dropped her hand and waited for Vidar's disapproval. It wasn't forthcoming. Instead he smiled and winced in pain at the same time. 'I would've given you a spanking had you but asked. You didn't need to go to this extreme to ensure that you received one.'

Her mouth dropped open and she was torn between laughing and blushing. 'I saved your life. You could be a little more grateful.'

He inclined his head and the smile dropped. 'Aye, that you did. Thank you, Wife. Thank you for saving me. You're a fine warrior.'

He meant it. His eyes were solemn and tender, and he didn't appear smug. He had finally called her a warrior. Her eyes pooled with tears. 'You're welcome.'

'I vow to you that I will try very hard to understand what that means for us. I never imagined a wife in my life, much less a wife like you. I hardly knew what to do with you at first. But I'm learning.'

She smiled. 'Me, too.' And her tears spilled down her cheeks. She'd never cried tears of happiness in her life, yet here they were.

He leaned down and kissed the droplets from her cheeks before dragging her mouth to his. 'I'm so grateful you're mine,' he whispered against her lips. 'I love you.'

She let out a soft cry as he pressed his lips to hers one more time. She was certain now that whatever they faced, they would face it together. That they would be one. 'Let's go home,' she said when they parted. Draping his arm around her shoulder, she helped him over to her horse to take him home.

'This doesn't absolve you from your spanking,' he teased.

She rolled her eyes. 'I wish you luck with that considering your cracked ribs.'

He laughed, but it turned into a soft groan of pain and she gave him a knowing glance. 'Oh, I can still spank you, you'll simply have to do the rest.'

Her belly fluttered and her mind started trying to conceive of all the delicious possibilities in his words. She could barely even fathom what he meant, but she knew that she'd enjoy figuring it out. 'I don't want you to worsen your injury.'

'You're right. We have time. Alvey and its future is ours.' His arm tightened and he pulled her closer to his side.

She closed her eyes and said a prayer of thanks that this Dane had been sent to her. With a little luck, the future of Alvey grew strong inside her even now.

* * * * *

*If you enjoyed this book,
you won't want to miss these other sexy
Viking stories from Harper St. George*

**ENSLAVED BY THE VIKING
ONE NIGHT WITH THE VIKING
IN BED WITH THE VIKING WARRIOR**

HOMETOWN HEARTS ♥

YES! Please send me **The Hometown Hearts Collection** in Larger Print. This collection begins with 3 FREE books and 2 FREE gifts in the first shipment. Along with my 3 free books, I'll also get the next 4 books from the Hometown Hearts Collection, in LARGER PRINT, which I may either return and owe nothing, or keep for the low price of $4.99 U.S./ $5.89 CDN each plus $2.99 for shipping and handling per shipment*. If I decide to continue, about once a month for 8 months I will get 6 or 7 more books, but will only need to pay for 4. That means 2 or 3 books in every shipment will be FREE! If I decide to keep the entire collection, I'll have paid for only 32 books because 19 books are FREE! I understand that accepting the 3 free books and gifts places me under no obligation to buy anything. I can always return a shipment and cancel at any time. My free books and gifts are mine to keep no matter what I decide.

262 HCN 3432 462 HCN 3432

Name	(PLEASE PRINT)	
Address		Apt. #
City	State/Prov.	Zip/Postal Code

Signature (if under 18, a parent or guardian must sign)

Mail to the **Reader Service:**
IN U.S.A.: P.O. Box 1867, Buffalo, NY. 14240-1867
IN CANADA: P.O. Box 609, Fort Erie, Ontario L2A 5X3

* Terms and prices subject to change without notice. Prices do not include applicable taxes. Sales tax applicable in NY. Canadian residents will be charged applicable taxes. This offer is limited to one order per household. All orders subject to approval. Credit or debit balances in a customer's account(s) may be offset by any other outstanding balance owed by or to the customer. Please allow 4 to 6 weeks for delivery. Offer available while quantities last. Offer not available to Quebec residents.

Your Privacy—The Reader Service is committed to protecting your privacy. Our Privacy Policy is available online at www.ReaderService.com or upon request from the Reader Service.

We make a portion of our mailing list available to reputable third parties that offer products we believe may interest you. If you prefer that we not exchange your name with third parties, or if you wish to clarify or modify your communication preferences, please visit us at www.ReaderService.com/consumerschoice or write to us at Reader Service Preference Service, P.O. Box 9062, Buffalo, NY. 14240-9062. Include your complete name and address.

HHBPA17

Get 2 Free Books,
Plus 2 Free Gifts—
just for trying the Reader Service!

HARLEQUIN
Western Romance

Get 2 Free Books,
Plus 2 Free Gifts—
just for trying the Reader Service!

YES! Please send me 2 FREE Harlequin Presents® novels and my 2 FREE gifts (gifts are worth about $10 retail). After receiving them, if I don't wish to receive any more books, I can return the shipping statement marked "cancel." If I don't cancel, I will receive 6 brand-new novels every month and be billed just $4.55 each for the regular-print edition or $5.55 each for the larger-print edition in the U.S., or $5.49 each for the regular-print edition or $5.99 each for the larger-print edition in Canada. That's a saving of at least 11% off the cover price! It's quite a bargain! Shipping and handling is just 50¢ per book in the U.S. and 75¢ per book in Canada.* I understand that accepting the 2 free books and gifts places me under no obligation to buy anything. I can always return a shipment and cancel at any time. The free books and gifts are mine to keep no matter what I decide.

Please check one: ☐ Harlequin Presents® Regular-Print   ☐ Harlequin Presents® Larger-Print
                              (106/306 HDN GLWL)   (176/376 HDN GLWL)

Name _____ (PLEASE PRINT) _____

Address _____ Apt. # _____

City _____ State/Prov. _____ Zip/Postal Code _____

Signature (if under 18, a parent or guardian must sign)

Mail to the Reader Service:

IN U.S.A.: P.O. Box 1341, Buffalo, NY 14240-8531
IN CANADA: P.O. Box 603, Fort Erie, Ontario L2A 5X3

Want to try two free books from another series?
Call 1-800-873-8635 or visit www.ReaderService.com.

* Terms and prices subject to change without notice. Prices do not include applicable taxes. Sales tax applicable in N.Y. Canadian residents will be charged applicable taxes. Offer not valid in Quebec. This offer is limited to one order per household. Books received may not be as shown. Not valid for current subscribers to Harlequin Presents books. All orders subject to approval. Credit or debit balances in a customer's account(s) may be offset by any other outstanding balance owed by or to the customer. Please allow 4 to 6 weeks for delivery. Offer available while quantities last.

Your Privacy—The Reader Service is committed to protecting your privacy. Our Privacy Policy is available online at www.ReaderService.com or upon request from the Reader Service.

We make a portion of our mailing list available to reputable third parties that offer products we believe may interest you. If you prefer that we not exchange your name with third parties, or if you wish to clarify or modify your communication preferences, please visit us at www.ReaderService.com/consumerschoice or write to us at Reader Service Preference Service, P.O. Box 9062, Buffalo, NY 14240-9062. Include your complete name and address.

HP17R2

Get 2 Free Books,
Plus 2 Free Gifts—
just for trying the Reader Service!